Don't miss the other books in
this gripping, sexy trilogy:

Diving In

In the Deep End

Also by Kate Cann

Footloose

Fiesta

Hard Cash

Shacked Up

Speeding

Escape

Sink or Swim

kate cann

■SCHOLASTIC

Scholastic Children's Books,
Commonwealth House, 1–19 New Oxford Street,
London WC1A 1NU, UK
a division of Scholastic Ltd
London ~ New York ~ Toronto ~ Sydney ~ Auckland
Mexico City ~ New Delhi ~ Hong Kong

First published in the UK by The Women's Press Ltd, 1998
This edition published by Scholastic Ltd, 2005

ISBN 0 439 96321 4

Typeset by M Rules
Printed and bound by Nørhaven Paperback A/S, Denmark

1 3 5 7 9 10 8 6 4 2

To Jeff

Chapter one

Everyone thought I coped brilliantly after Art dumped me. And I did – I functioned really well. A soggy, grief-stricken month or two and then, when I found he'd disappeared off to the other side of the world and there was no chance of just bumping into him somewhere, I felt a line had been drawn, and I got on with my life. I threw myself into my work. I walked, talked, went out, ate food. Even laughed, occasionally, although inside my head it sounded like an echo.

My friends approved of the way I'd come through it. We were all very hot on girl strength in our group, and mooning around after some git who'd let you down was seen as a definite weakness. And Mum was actually proud of me. It was like I'd been blooded on my first hunt, and survived with honour.

"No, she's fine," I overheard her telling some cronies at one of their gatherings round our kitchen table. "She's revising, she's seeing her friends – frankly, I think she's all the stronger for it."

"No one new on the scene yet then?" someone put in.

"Good God, no. Last thing Colette wants is another male in her life, with A levels so close. No –

it's all back to how it was before now."

"Well, not quite, Justine," someone else piped up. "I mean – how can it be. You know."

"I know WHAT, Angela?"

"Um. I mean – they – I mean they were pretty involved, weren't they?"

"You mean they had a sexual relationship," said Mum, heavily. "Yes, they did. But things are different nowadays, Angela. Girls don't get so . . . SILLY about things. Not like we did. They take things in their stride."

"Oh, come on Justine, human nature doesn't change, human nature—"

"Angela – really. Colette's fine. She's put it all down to experience, and moved on."

There was a long pause, broken only by the pouring out of more wine. I shuffled off upstairs.

So there you are, Art, I thought. *Mum Has Spoken. You're not the great love of my life, you're just experience, OK? You're a learning curve, that's all. So get out of my head, you bastard. Get out of my soul. Leave me alone.*

But he wouldn't. He kept coming back. Especially when I lay down in the dark to sleep. I remembered the weight of him, the way his skin felt, the smell of his hair, the taste of him, and I hurt with loneliness, with wanting him.

I'd lie there at night and fantasize endlessly about

why he'd gone. I knew – I *knew* – some of the reason was what had been growing between us. I knew he'd been scared by it. We'd come through some really fierce times together, and you can't do that without a strong link being forged. We'd opened up to each other in ways we'd never opened up to anyone before. He was the first, the only guy I'd ever slept with. And the sex had been. . . I didn't want to think about how amazing it had been. How it had transformed everything, all the time we spent together, like some kind of secret, like wonderful music.

So I'd lie there and picture him sitting alone on a deserted beach, or alone in a crowded bar, gazing tearfully at the sunset, or into his glass, until suddenly with a great heart-tearing burst of emotion he realized it was me he wanted after all, me for ever and always. And then he'd leap to his feet and get the next plane back and come to find me, not stopping for anything . . . sometimes I had him practically *swimming* from New Zealand to get to me . . . and then, and then. . .

And then finally, I'd drift off to sleep. Only that didn't help, because of the dreams I had. Jesus, the dreams. We'd be following each other, circling each other, prowling round each other, at a party, or in the woods, or anywhere, and I'd see his face so clearly, and all I wanted was to touch him, get hold of him. And then I did get hold of him and we'd make love, fantastically, wonderfully, and I'd wake up wanting to howl with loss.

It made me really sick at myself, the way I couldn't just throw him off. I started to think there was something wrong with me. I mean – just how long does anyone need to get over a relationship? Even their first real relationship. Six months had to be enough. I was doing what you're supposed to do. I was getting out, getting on – taking exercise and not taking drugs, only drinking when I really felt I had to. It just wasn't fair. I was making an effort, honestly I was, but it wasn't working.

And the thing is, I couldn't even talk to anyone about it, not any more. I'd had my allowable grieving period. To suddenly try to tell people that – hey, I'm not actually over him at all, I'm only alive when I'm reliving how we used to be together – nobody would have wanted to hear. It would be too scary to listen to. You're not supposed to feel things that long, let them chew you up that badly.

The way I see it is this. Some old lady's husband dies. Everyone's very sympathetic at first, very supportive, handing across hankies, ready with the arm round the shoulders. And then the sympathy gets less, and people start expecting you to pull yourself together a bit more. And you have to, or you cross some kind of thin line between what's OK and what's not OK. One side of the line you're just grieving very bad, the other side you're a total loony, lost in misery. You keep his photo on the shelf, nicely dusted, maybe even a vase of flowers next to it – that's nice. That's remembering, keeping his memory. But you start talking to him in the kitchen and making his favourite cakes and laying out his pyjamas and putting a cup of cocoa next to his empty chair – and you're a total loony. Time to get help.

And I was the teen equivalent. I'd crossed the thin line. I was right there with the loonies, making the cocoa, talking to the emptiness. Art was more real to me still, far more real, than all the stuff actually happening to me, out there in life. How *do* you move on, when all you want to do is go back? Sometimes I felt the pain hadn't got less over those six months – it had got worse. It had all crystallized down into a little despairing knot in my stomach that never seemed to go away.

But I'd played the heroic getting-on-with-my-life bit so well and for so long that there was no way I could let anyone know what was happening underneath. Because then they'd know how fake she was, that Coll they saw, the one who'd got over him. And I was scared of admitting she was fake. I was scared of what would happen if I did.

I needed help, but no one was going to know it. No one needed to know it, because I was functioning so well.

Chapter two

It was my best friend Val who had the first doubts about me and my "recovery". She started to insist on me going out with her and her boyfriend Greg on a real regular basis, to the pub, to films. Sometimes there'd be a whole crowd of us, sometimes there'd be just the three of us. At first I'd managed to fob her off, tell her I was working or wanting to see something on telly, but then she began to get this knowing, disapproving look on her face, and said things like "Come on Coll, don't make excuses. You should get out more."

No one wants a picture of themselves as a sad loner who hardly ever goes out, so it was easy for her to persuade me into going along. And really, I should have been grateful to have such a loyal friend as Val. But going out with her and Greg made me feel like topping myself.

It wasn't just that it depressed me, going back to what I'd done before Art had come on the scene. And it wasn't envy of their happy coupledom, I swear it wasn't. You couldn't envy them, the way they were.

Just over eight months ago now, Val had had an abortion. Greg had been consumed with guilt over it, taken it upon himself as his fault. You got the feeling from him that nothing he could do for Val would ever make up for it, and nothing awful she could do to him would ever be as bad as what she'd had to go through. He'd stick by her, whatever, now. In a way, I understood the way he felt, but it didn't lead to a healthy relationship.

There'd be maybe six of you, in the pub, having a conversation and all the time there was this other conversation going on in code between Val and Greg. This conversation had nothing to do with what everyone else was talking about; it was about their relationship. Val would dig at Greg, and make nasty, pointed comments, and he'd snap back, or leave pointed silences, and it was all about bitterness, and resentment, and disappointment. It was horrible to sit through. Sometimes they'd remind me of two animals trapped in a cage together, tearing lumps off each other. But they both knew when to stop before the damage got too bad. It never got to be a real row. Val would sit back, pouting, and say, "Jesus, Greg, you have been in a *foul mood* all evening. What on *earth's* the matter?" And this was Greg's cue to somehow force down all that he was thinking and feeling and grunt, "Yeah. Sorry, love."

They were both bored and frustrated with each other, but they didn't seem to even consider splitting up. And they seemed to have silently made this agreement that, because of what she'd been through, Val could erupt and let out her anger but Greg had to sit on his, otherwise the whole thing would go up in flames.

I was positive they should finish it, but I knew better than to say anything. I'd tried to talk about it once with Rachel, after an evening full of poisonous undercurrent from the pair of them, but it was pretty clear right away that she thought I wasn't seeing things straight.

"Oh, they'll work it out," she'd said. "Every couple has its bad patches."

"Yeah, but this bad patch has been going on for *ever*," I'd replied. "I mean – they're just going round and round in circles, making each other miserable – they'd be much better off just to take a deep breath and finish it."

"Well – I think it's good they're not just giving up on it. If everyone just cleared off at the first sign of trouble, no one would stay together, would they."

"But staying together when it's like that! It has to be better to be on your own."

Rachel fixed me with a knowing look. "Look, Coll, everyone has their own kind of relationship. OK, theirs isn't much fun at the moment – but at least it's real."

I shut up. That meant – Your relationship with Art wasn't real. You can't judge. I knew they all thought I was duped by Art. Because he'd treated me so badly in the beginning; because of the way I'd been obsessed by him. They thought it was some kind of fake fantasy. Well, maybe they were right. But when I sat listening to Greg and Val snapping and snarling at each other, I couldn't help thinking fantasy had rather a lot going for it.

Val stepped up her campaign to socialize me. "You're turning into a bloody nun," she said. "You never want to do anything."

"Val, that's not true. I went out with you all last week."

"Yeah – to a film. Big social event, Coll. And you'll come to the pub and chew the fat about Life and crap. But any mention of a party or a club – forget it."

"Yeah, OK. I just don't feel like it, Val. I mean – it's OK at the start. But then the lights go low and guys start sniffing round, trying to give you mouth-to-mouth – I mean, it's *sordid*. It pisses me off."

There was a pause, during which Val's mouth formed itself into an I've-just-been-proved-right smirk. "You see?" she said. "A *nun*. You bloody are, Coll. Just tell me the last time you got off with anyone?"

I frowned, as though I was trying to remember, trying to sort out the exact last guy from all the ranks and ranks I'd been pulling in the last few days. "We . . . ell. . ."

"Don't give me *we . . . ll.* At Carol's party, you hid in the bog half the evening, didn't you."

"Yeah, but you *saw* that geek who was after me—"

"And a couple of weeks ago – leaving the club to go home early—"

"Val, I had a really bad headache. I told you. Practically a migraine."

Val snorted. "I *give up* with you! You never used to be like this. You know – there *are* other blokes in the world. Other than Mr Incredibly-Gorgeous-Can't-Cope-With-Involvement Johnson."

I smiled. "Yeah, I know."

"I mean – it's like you've switched off or something. From guys."

"Well, I –" For one heady moment, I was tempted to tell her. But I couldn't. She was looking so critical. "I just don't want to get all screwed up again," I muttered. "Not yet."

"Coll. For God's sake. No one said anything about getting all heavy. I mean – you've *done* heavy. I just mean you could have a bit of fun, now and then."

"It's just I – I never seem to fancy anyone, I never feel – I dunno. I never see the *point*."

"Oh, blimey. Art can't have been that good."

"He was."

Val gave me one of her looks. Half disapproving, and half downright jealous. "OK, OK. Lucky you. But now you have a choice. You can cut everyone else out and devote your life to remembering how amazing he was – or you can try and get *over* it."

"I *am* over it! That's not fair, Val. Everyone says how well—"

"Oh, sure. We're not mopping you up every five minutes any more. I mean *really* over it."

Tell her, I thought, again. What are best friends for?

They're for lecturing you, that's what for. She was off again. "I mean – I just think you should start trying to have some *fun*, OK, Coll? Maybe even let someone else touch you once in a while? I mean – has your mouth become some kind of *shrine* to that sad git, or what?"

I laughed. "Oh, come on. It's not that easy to just – I mean, I know it's been a long time but – well, how would *you* feel if you and Greg split and everyone started telling you –"

Just for a minute, Val's face took on a really hard expression. "I wouldn't take the time over it you're taking, believe me. Now. This party on Saturday. Mike's eighteenth. And I happen to know he has stacks of gorgeous cousins. And you're coming."

I didn't argue. Firstly because I didn't have the energy, and secondly, because I knew Val was only giving me such a hard time because she cared about me, and some of me was grateful and even thought she was probably right. I was becoming a nun – a sad, boring, past-fixated nun. Saturday night I spent a long time in the bathroom, showering and creaming myself up, fixing my make-up. I told myself that tonight, I was going to pull. I was going to score, and it would be my cure. Maybe if I kissed someone other than Art, I'd wipe the memory away a bit. I was quite clinical about it.

I got out one of my favourite dresses, a dress Art used to love – OK, OK, who *cares* if he used to love it. It was aubergine-coloured, short and quite tight, but it had a sporty feel – you could move in it. I'd worn it with bare legs last summer, but that night I put it on with dark tights and these new, high shoes I'd bought the weekend before. Then I went down to the landing and looked in the long mirror there, and I got a surprise, because I liked myself. Kind of objectively, I liked myself. When I'd first met Art I used to be so worried I wasn't good enough, attractive enough, and then, when we were sleeping together, it was like this intoxication, as though I was so alive, so beautiful, every inch of me. And now – I just knew I looked all right. A bit strained round the eyes, maybe, a bit distant, but all right. I put on some lipstick and smiled over Val calling my mouth a shrine. *Not any more*, I thought. *Time to get desecrated.*

* * *

12

Greg and Val drove up to collect me at about twenty to nine, and we headed off to the party. In the car, they made bright, cheerful conversation; I think they'd been discussing me and decided I needed some social encouragement. It was sweet and incredibly painful at the same time.

I felt very cool and collected as we walked into the party. It was in quite a big house and it was already very crowded. Greg and Val were being all protective, shepherding me into the kitchen, finding me a drink, smiling at me in a manic sort of way that meant I had to smile back, but soon I managed to convince them I felt fine, and they drifted off together, and left me alone.

I'd been to a few parties in the last few months, but this was different. Before, I'd had my armour on. Casual, loose clothes and lots of "don't look at me, don't talk to me, I'm not really here" vibes. Now – I don't know what messages I was giving off. Something like cold determination, probably. There were quite a few unattached blokes drifting around, and one or two gave me the eye, and I looked back. I wandered around, talking to people I knew, going in and out of the kitchen, refilling my glass. Waiting.

Then there was a space when I just stood against a wall and watched everyone. I'd never have done that before, before Art. I'd never have had the nerve. But tonight I felt almost sure of myself. *There's nothing I don't know now*, I said in my head. *Nothing.* It gave me a kind of pleasure, to think that. A bit double-edged, because it reminded me what I was missing, but a kind of pleasure all the same.

Two lads were leaning up against the wall opposite me, across the other side of the room, and I knew they were talking about me, the way they kept glancing over. Being looked at like that was beginning to make my neck prickle. *Maybe it's just sex you're missing*, I said to myself. *Art's the only guy you've ever slept with, so you kind of think he* is *sex. Maybe if you. . .* One of the guys had peeled off from the other and wandered over. He stood in front of me, head on one side.

"You on your own?" he asked. He was blond, a bit sleazy-looking.

"Yes," I said. "Well – I came with some friends, but they've cleared off somewhere."

"Yeah?" He smiled, knowingly. "Upstairs?"

"Maybe." *Don't try and embarrass me, you wanker.* "Or the shrubbery."

He laughed. "Need a drink?"

"Yeah. Why not." He turned and went into the kitchen, and I followed him. He was a bit taller than me, chunky, with a confident walk. I could tell from his back view he was dying to make some kind of signal of triumph to his mate.

You'll do, I thought.

Chapter three

We went into the kitchen and he made a big joke out of finding a clean glass for me, saying how diseases can be transmitted by glass as well as all sorts of other things, hor, hor. As he was talking I was scanning his face, trying to convince myself that it would be OK to get off with him. He had a nice mouth, large but not too full, and good teeth, straight and clean-looking.

"So," he was saying, "you haven't told me your name yet. Mine's Lee."

"Coll."

"Hi, Coll," he said, then he smirked at me, one eyebrow going all crinkly like James Bond or something.

Don't, I thought. *Don't be too much of an idiot, or I won't be able to go through with this.*

"Who d'you know here, then?" he went on.

"I came with Val – she knows Mike. Well, her boyfriend does."

"I'm Mike's cousin."

"Ah. Yeah, I was told there were going to be a lot of cousins here."

He blethered on about Mike and the party and

what he did and who he knew. He was running on an anxious desire for there not to be any kind of silence between us. I wondered if it was as boring for him as it was for me. Then he shut up, and jerked his head towards the party room, eyebrows raised. I nodded, and headed for the door. He followed, close. I could tell he was thinking about putting his arm round me. I could sense it, rising and falling behind my back like a train signal gone mad.

The room had got darker, some slow music was playing, and I felt this great weight of dreary inevitability settle on me. *Get on with it*, I told myself sternly. *Go through with it.* I walked a little way into the room, then I turned right round to face him, smiling, and put my arms round his waist.

He seemed a bit taken aback, but at least it stopped him starting up with more chat. We swayed about a bit together, him brushing my hair with his cheek, moving his hands on my back. This stupid, rejecting feeling was flooding into me, and I could feel myself wanting to bolt, so I deliberately lifted my face up to his, and didn't move it when his mouth dropped down on mine. He stopped dancing, then, and wrapped his arms tightly round me, and got into a serious clinch.

After a minute or so, I pushed him gently away. Far more gently than I wanted to push him. In fact, it took a great effort of will not to shove him backwards so hard he hit the wall.

"What's up?" he murmured.

"Nothing," I lied. "It's a bit . . . it's a bit public, that's all." He breathed down on me heavily, smoochily. "So shall we go somewhere less public?"

I half shook my head, and Lee slid his arms round me again. I made myself put my arms back round him, then I forced myself to reach up and kiss him again. I felt his tongue slither over mine and I gagged silently.

I pushed him away again, and stepped backwards.

You're wrong, you're all wrong. You smell wrong and you taste wrong. You have a little soft roll round your waist where it should be hard; your hands are too small, they're not holding me right. Your mouth doesn't move right, it doesn't feel right.

You're not Art.

"Look – what's up?" Lee said again. He sounded a bit miffed, this time, and I couldn't blame him.

I took a deep breath. "Nothing. I – look, I'm sorry."

"You kissed me then," he accused.

"I – I know. I'm sorry."

"I said let's go somewhere else, but you—"

"I *know*. Look – I'm – I'm all messed up, right now. I think I'd better go."

"Hey, no need for that." He was suddenly concerned, kindly. "Just . . . tell me about it.

17

"I – no. Please. I'm sorry. I just – look, I need another drink."

"Sure," he said, putting his arm round me and steering me towards the kitchen.

I smiled fixedly at him as he handed me a plastic cup full of urine-coloured wine. I felt ashamed. After all, it wasn't his fault. *Sorry*, I said to him, silently. *It's just you're not* him, *and kissing is him, it's him. Sex is him.* I felt like I wanted to break down there and then and start howling. I choked down a mouthful of wine and said I had to go to the loo.

"There's one through there," Lee said, pointing towards the other side of the kitchen. "It used to be an outside one, but they've tacked it on to the house."

Outside one, outside one, I chanted idiotically, as I made my way through a skinny little utility room piled up with laundry and tins of cat food. Outside, outside. It was where I most wanted to be. I found the loo, had a quick pee, and turned to go back into the kitchen, but my legs wouldn't move forward. I stood there, hands in fists, heart pounding. Then I tried the back door. It was open. I stepped through it; a security light flashed, lighting up willow trees and shrubs and a garden fence.

With a gate in it.

You have a choice, I said to myself, as I walked towards it. You either go in and face Lee and apologize to him and have him ask you what the problem is and try to explain without bursting into tears and try to get away and find Val and Greg and explain to them and get your coat and leave in a sensible fashion – or you avoid all that and run.

I ran.

Chapter four

I was so relieved just to be out of it. So relieved to be acting on pure instinct, the instinct to escape. My mind was empty. I could feel all kinds of guilt and doubt hammering at the edges, waiting to get a foothold, but for the moment it was just beautifully empty, and the cold air on my face felt good. I power-walked along, arms pumping, telling myself I sort of knew where I was and I was pretty sure this was the right direction to take me home.

But ten minutes along the empty suburban street, and I hadn't got anywhere I recognized. The street seemed to go on for miles; all the houses looked the same. And worse, my adrenalin was beginning to ebb, and the embarrassment and misery was kicking in.

Brilliant, I muttered to myself, just fab. I'd wanted a cure, I'd wanted to wash the taste of Art away with someone else, and all I'd done was make it worse, make me miss him worse. I couldn't even *kiss* that guy. And I acted like some sort of a hysterical prat, running out like that. *What'll everyone think of me?*

It's the sort of thing you do when you're losing it, I thought, as I tottered on in my stupid high heels, feet

aching, heart aching. *That's what they'll think.*
Maybe I am losing it. But oh, God, I can't go back to
meaningless gropes with strangers. I can't. What I
had with Art was total. Mind, body, spirit. Love.
Even if it wasn't that way for him. I can't just—

A car had screeched to a stop alongside me and
now a couple of shorn heads were craning alarmingly
far out of the driver's window.

"Hello, darling. Ain't you cold wivout a coat?"

I gawped moronically.

"Want a lift?"

"No thanks – I live just up there," I lied, pointing
vaguely ahead.

"Your loss, sweetheart!" They revved off.

I quickened my pace and turned a corner into
another tree-lined road, indistinguishable from the
first, and admitted to myself that if I was right about
where I was, I should have hit the town by now.
Which meant I wasn't right about where I was.
Which meant I was lost.

I checked my watch: 11.30. If I found a phone
booth, I could call home. I could tell Mum – *what*
could I tell her? "Hi, Mum – I ran out in the street
'cos someone tried to snog me and I don't know
where I am but can you come and pick me up?" I
didn't think so. I'd have to find my way back to the
party and phone from there. Only then I'd risk
meeting up with Lee again, and having to. . .

Another car squealed to a halt right next to me, hooting its horn, and before I could react Val had leaped from the passenger seat and confronted me. "Coll, you *idiot*!" she screeched. "What on earth are you playing at? What did you just *clear off* for?"

I gazed at her, stunned, silent. All around me, I could sense bedroom curtains being pulled back and people peering indignantly down into the street. "Everyone was *really worried*," she ranted on. "Just going without telling anyone! Lee thought you were *on* something or something!"

Greg leaned out of the car window and said, "Get in, OK?"

Thankfully, I pulled the car door open and scrambled in the back seat. Val got in the front, then twisted round and carried on yelling at me. "I don't know *what* you think you were playing at. Lee's really nice – he's a great bloke. He said he waited for ages, he thought you were ill or something, and then he looked everywhere for you – you had half the *party* looking everywhere for you—"

"Great," I muttered. "Just great."

"Well what the hell d'you expect us to do?" she practically screamed. "You go off, you don't tell anyone, you get yourself lost, *don't* pretend you weren't lost—"

"I'm sorry," I croaked. "I just – I just had to get out—"

"*Why*? Why did you?"

"I felt – I felt awful, and—"

"*You* felt awful? How d'you think Lee felt?"

"Val, for God's sake," murmured Greg. "It wasn't that much of a big deal."

She glared at him, then me. "You're really different, Coll, you know that? You've changed."

"Val – I just – I panicked."

"You *panicked*? What *about*, for Christ's sake? You're becoming a real weirdo. Jesus. You didn't even take your coat."

"Val – just leave it, can't you?" said Greg.

She turned to him, spitting. "Why the hell *should* I leave it?"

"Because if she ran off – it's because she's upset – and you're not even—"

"I'm not even *what*?"

"Listening to her."

"*Listening* to her? I've done nothing *but* listen to her! I'm sick of it. I mean – *Christ*. She's either like some ghost hanging around in the corners, or she's throwing fits or something—"

"Val, shut up," said Greg. He sounded tired, bone tired. Val twisted away from him, furious.

"I'm really sorry," I muttered, again, from the back seat. What else could I say? *I'm sorry I messed up. I'm sorry you yell at me and don't listen to me. I'm sorry I can't tell you the truth any more.*

We travelled the last few miles in silence, pulled up outside my house and I said thank you, then I said goodnight. Greg smiled, Val half-smiled.

I slunk upstairs and lay on the bed and then I just started sobbing, real chest-heaving sobs, so loud I had to stuff my duvet in my mouth in case Mum or Dad heard. I'd failed, I'd failed. I'd made everything worse – I'd ripped everything open and missing Art was like agony now.

And Val's right, I thought, *I'm becoming a real weirdo. She saw the real Coll tonight, the sad mad one, and she hates her, and I don't blame her, I hate her too.*

I'll get stuck like this. Growing older, staying the same, fixated on grief, still wanting Art back, never having fun, ruining parties, losing friends.

I knew I should talk to someone about it, maybe even someone professional, but I was afraid to. If I talked about this inside-Coll, if I even admitted to her existence to someone else it would – I don't know – let her out, somehow. Give her more power.

Christ, I really am going insane. Schizophrenic. Somehow I've got to keep that capable, coping Coll up front or I'll just lose it.

I stared at the ceiling and thought how I'd phone Val tomorrow and try to put things right. Just tell her *sorry, sorry, sorry, I lost it for a bit but I'm OK now.* I was past grieving for the fact that I couldn't be straight with her any more, open and honest like we used to be. I just had to keep the pretence going.

I got up and peeled off my dress, let it fall on the floor, crawled back under the duvet and switched off the lamp beside my bed. And I let Art come in like an incubus, like a ghost that was robbing me of my life.

Chapter five

"I mean, honestly, Coll," Val said crisply on the other end of the phone line. "This just isn't like you. Getting *this* screwed up – over a *guy*."

"Yeah, I know," I appeased her. "It was – I dunno, some kind of weird flashback. I'd had too much to drink and then when I kissed Lee I just—"

"I mean – when are you going to get *over* it? It's crazy. It's been six months!"

"Look – I know. Forget it. Please. I am over it. Really."

"Well act it, then! You're worth so much more than that Johnson *git*. You are, really. And Lee would've been good for you. He's your sort. He's. . ." She rambled on, lecturing, and I wanted to scream at her – *D'you think I'm choosing this?* But I didn't. Better for her to think it was a blip, a mistake, not to be repeated.

"You just have to hang in there," she was saying, sounding kinder. "Next weekend Caro and I are going clubbing. Just us, no blokes. You can come. And the week after that – it's Ben's party. He's great. And he's got *great* friends. You've got in a rut, Coll. You need more fun, that's all."

Fun with Val. It was like some kind of life sentence. Worse, it was like some kind of a test. The vision of a dark, flickering club rose in front of me, with Val leaping about, flirting and proving she wasn't tied down to Greg and bullying me into getting off with someone – and I wanted to be sick. I couldn't go through with it, I knew that. I just didn't know what excuse I could come up with this time.

The next day at school, news of my behaviour had got round from a couple of girls who'd been at the party. Everyone was ghoulishly interested in the fact that the girl who had apparently coped so well with being ditched had suddenly freaked out. Val was tight-lipped about it at first, then gradually drawn into giving her theory on my problems. She even wanted me to join in discussing it, like some kind of gruesome telly-confessional. I think she thought if everyone publicly agreed how daft I was being, I'd somehow be *shamed* into getting back to normal.

At break, the gorgeous Samantha passed me a copy of one of her girly magazines, open at a page that said "Unbreak your Heart: Twenty Ways to Get Over Him Leaving". I smiled at her in a sickly fashion, took the mag, and glanced through it. There was a picture of someone hacking up a photo of a lad at the top, and then a list. Have a hot bath with candles round the edge. See a film you wouldn't normally see. Start a new exercise regime and this time stick to it. Enrol at night school. Take a weekend break and walk ten miles. Get into yoga. Get into massage. Invite Someone Different Round and Cook in a Wok.

It was all supposed to work in a matter of weeks – days even. They had to be kidding. A bit of me had thought there might be something in it that would help, but this was a joke. I didn't need top tips, clearly. I needed something more drastic, like a personality transplant. And more urgently, I really, really needed an excuse to get out of Val's Saturday night.

Every night after school that week, I went straight home and shut myself away in my room, telling Mum I was going to work. I did do some, but I also spent a lot of time just lying on the bed, watching the night come in, and thinking how many different shades of dark there are in the sky. Often I'd doze off, wanting the escape of sleep.

Mum was quietly pleased with me and all the effort she thought I was putting into my revision. She'd get a bit concerned when she saw how little I wanted to eat at suppertime but when I lied and told her I'd had some fruit earlier she'd say OK then. It's amazing what you can hide from the people close to you when things seem to be going the way they want them to go.

Chapter six

Synchronicity. Serendipity. I believe in them, seriously. Thursday night in a kind of doomed panic, dreading the weekend when I was going to have to appear to be having fun, I left the house for a walk and found myself heading into the centre of town. It was late night shopping, and there were lots of people rotating about, clutching carrier bags. And I saw the notice that was going to save me.

It was stuck to the inside of the window of a new cappuccino and ice-cream bar, all bright green ink and silver underlining, and it said:

Wanted: Saturday Night Help.
6 pm to 11 pm shift.
Good Pay. Tips

I took in a deep breath, checked my reflection in the window, uttered a brief prayer of thanks that I had my new jumper on and washed my hair the night before, and pushed the door open. Desperation makes you brave.

A girl with cropped, blonde-red hair and weird green eyes watched me as I approached the gleaming marble counter. "Yes?" she said.

"Ah . . . um. It's the notice you have in the—"

"Bill!" she yelled. "Someone about the job!"

I swallowed nervously, and a man appeared through the heavy bead curtains at the back, drying his hands on a tea-towel. He was about thirty, skinny, studiously cool.

"Hi," I said, "I saw your notice and—"

"Great. Let's sit over there." He ushered me over to a little wrought iron table in the corner, overshadowed by a big, leafy plant, and we sat down. "Now. You are—"

"Colette. Coll."

"And are you at college or—"

"School. St Catherine's. I'm doing A levels."

"Ah. So you're – how old?"

"Seventeen."

"And have you ever done this kind of work before?"

"Er – no. But I do stuff at home. I mean – I can make sandwiches and, er, scoop out ice-cream and stuff."

He sat back in his chair, folded his arms, and stared at me. "Like a coffee?" he asked.

"Um – yes. Yes, please."

"Maggie!" he shouted. "Bring us over a coupla cappuccinos, would you, darling?"

There was a long pause, during which he surveyed

me, and I tried not to shift about too much on my seat. Then he leaned towards me again. "OK, Colette . . . Coll. You're doing A levels – you're obviously bright. You can give the right change, and learn how to use the coffee machine. But we're looking for something a bit more here."

"A bit more. . .?" I repeated moronically.

"He means you've got to look good," said Maggie, appearing suddenly beside us. "Act charming. He's a sexist shit."

"Get lost, Maggie," he laughed. "That rule applies to young men too."

"You bet it does," she gurgled, plonking down the coffees. *Especially* young men." She had a great voice, soft-vowelled, northern – too big for her small frame.

"Get lost," repeated Bill, pleasantly, and she wandered off, laughing. Bill turned back to me. "When she says act charming and all that – it's just . . . this is a smart place, Colette. We want smart people working here. Can I see your nails?"

Dumbly, I held out my hands. My nails were pale, unpainted – positively nun-like. "Great," he said." Don't like 'em bitten, or red claws. OK. Can you wear your hair tied back? And maybe a bit more make-up, yeah?"

I nodded, dumbly. I wasn't wearing any make-up, so that wouldn't be too hard.

"Great? Trial run Saturday?"

I licked my dry lips, smiled, and nodded again. This was too easy. "Thanks," I stuttered. "Brilliant. So – six o'clock?"

Bill laughed. "Haven't you forgotten something? Like pay?"

I blinked. I didn't think he needed to hear that getting a Saturday night job had nothing to do with money and everything to do with getting Val off my back.

"It's twenty quid," he went on. "And the nicer you are the more tips you take home. OK. See you Saturday."

Maggie grinned at me as I left, and I found myself grinning back. "See you Saturday," she said.

"Are you doing that shift too?" I asked.

"Yeah," she said. Then she winked.

Chapter seven

"I still think you're weird," Val grumbled. "Six to eleven on a Saturday, for God's sake. That's party time. Who wants to work then?"

"Yeah, I know." I moved over to her dressing table, and rearranged her nail varnishes for her. "But I've been thinking, Val – I really want to get some cash together, for after the exams. I want to go somewhere – you know, get out of here, travel."

"Fine – but why a Saturday *night* job?"

"There's more of them going," I improvised. "No one wants to work then – like you said." Well, for all I knew it was true.

"Where are you planning on going, anyway?"

"Dunno yet. Egypt. Israel." I was a bit vague, but then I'd only just thought it up. "Maybe just a holiday – maybe I'll do a gap year. What about you?"

"I dunno." Val subsided on to her bed and looked gloomy. "It depends. We haven't decided. About university, or having a year off, or anything."

I looked at her. *You mean* you *haven't decided*, I thought. *Poor old Greg won't even get a vote.* I studied her as she slouched on the bed, edgily picking at her nails. If she hadn't gone through with the abortion, the baby would be on the verge of getting itself born right now. I wondered how much she dwelt on that thought, or whether she'd banned it from her mind.

I certainly wasn't going to bring it up. "I'm sorry about missing your clubbing session this Saturday," I lied. "It would've been good."

"I don't know if we're still going," Val said. "Greg and I had a real bust-up over it."

"Why?"

"Because he got all martyred and pathetic about it. He didn't really want me to go."

"I s'pose . . . I s'pose he felt a bit left out?" I ventured. "Saturday night, and all."

Val's eyes narrowed, and her mouth went into that thin, mean line I was seeing more and more frequently nowadays. "I just wanted some *fun*," she said. "I mean – I find it quite incredible that he can't *trust* me."

"Yeah, but he doesn't go out much on his own, maybe he felt—"

"Well, that's his decision! God, I get *sick* of him sometimes . . . he's like some great *weight*—"

I took in a deep breath. "Well, why don't you finish it then?"

"Oh, Coll, for God's sake! You don't just give up on . . . I mean, it's not like I *always* feel like that. Sometimes I love the feeling that we're together. That he's always there for me – that we want the same thing. But at the same time – I dunno, it's *crazy*. We act like we're settled down or something, like we'll be together for ever."

"But that must make you feel kind of safe," I answered, a bit wistfully.

"Yeah, I s'pose. But if you're safe you're . . . limited too, right? No chance of change. Oh *God*, I don't know." She threw herself backwards on the bed and crossed her arms behind her head, gazing up at the ceiling. "You know we both had offers from Sheffield Uni," she went on. "Well, he's kind of putting it all on me. He keeps saying – I want what you want. And sometimes I feel so scared of the thought of going to university I just want him along too. But then – maybe that's the wrong reason to want him along."

"But Val – it's not the *only* reason you'd want him along. . .?"

She didn't answer, just rolled over on her side and announced how tired she was. I looked at my watch, and told her I'd leave her to have a nap.

"Thanks," she mumbled, tugging the duvet over her legs.

I stood for a minute, just watching her lying there. I had this horrible, aching lonely feeling inside me. Val and I used to be so close – and now there was this great gulf between us, uncrossable.

She's scared of me, I thought, with a kind of dreary recognition. *She's scared of my unhappiness – scared of ending up like me, maybe.*

I turned to go.

"Hey – if I'm just stuck with Greg this Saturday," she called after me, "maybe we'll drop in on you at your coffee bar."

Don't, I thought. "OK," I said.

Saturday afternoon arrived, and I began to feel really nervous at the prospect of working in the café that evening. The only money I'd ever earned before had been from baby-sitting and delivering circulars, and that hardly counted as breaking into the world of work. Well, this didn't count either, really, but at least it was a real job. I showered; I remembered what Maggie had been wearing and pulled on clean jeans and a loose shirt. Then I put on a bit of subtle eye make-up and lots of lipstick and tied back my hair in a big, heavy plait.

Maggie was behind the counter when I arrived at the coffee bar. She didn't see me right away; she was slicing up a couple of baguettes, making sandwiches. Most of the tables were full, with carrier bags crowding out the floor.

I went up to the counter, and said, "Hi, Maggie."

She spun round. "Hi! Wrong side, Coll."

I smiled, and walked round to join her.

"This is the end of shopping lot," she said. "It'll quieten down in a bit, and then I'll show you how to work the cappuccino machine before all the Night Creatures appear."

I laughed. "D'you get many of them?"

"Yeah – off and on. Mostly just for cappuccino and ice-cream, but you still get the odd hungry geezer in or someone who's too tight to take his sort out for a proper meal." She started rummaging in a drawer, and pulled out a brown, gold and white striped butcher's apron. "Here. Your uniform. Just like mine." She leaned forward, and hung it round my neck. "Gorge. Goes with your hair."

Two middle-aged women came in and plumped themselves down at a table. "Betterware!" one of them was insisting. "Can't get better oven-gloves than those."

"But the man doesn't come any more. . ." wailed her friend.

"Phone head office! *Make* him come! They're pretty, and they *last*, and you can just stick 'em in the machine. . ."

"Go on," smiled Maggie. "Take their order."

Feeling very self-conscious, I walked over and stood by the two women's table, then I cleared my throat and squeaked, "What would you like?"

"An extension on my credit card, love. And two teas."

"Ah – right."

I crept back to Maggie, and hissed, "Do we *do* teas?"

"Yup. Darjeeling, Earl Grey, and Bog Standard. Otherwise known as 'Proper Tea'. Which they will want, so don't bother to go back and ask."

Minutes later, I was conveying two steaming cups to the women's table, they thanked me, and I went back behind the counter with an almost ludicrous sense of achievement. Then Maggie pointed out that two tables had paid their bills and left, so I cleared the tables, stacked the crocks and took them into the tiny kitchen behind the curtain. Then I went back to the tables and wiped them down. When I got back behind the counter Maggie showed me how the cappuccino machine worked, how to master the hot froth technique, and exactly how much chocolate or cinnamon to sprinkle on top.

As soon as we'd done that, a whole group of loud kids burst through the door, making a big fuss about ordering ice-cream cones and whether to be real pigs and have doubles and making sexy innuendoes about chocolate flakes. I helped Maggie scoop the cones out and took the money, and as I slammed the till shut I realized I felt something weird, something I hadn't felt for a long time. Happy.

Chapter eight

We were really busy for the next two hours. Mostly ice-cream, because the café already had a reputation for selling the best in town. The customers got louder and friendlier, because they had a few drinks inside them. I kept expecting Bill to turn up, but Maggie said he often just left it to her. "I'm good, you see," she grinned. "Re-spon-sible. And he has this other place, a few miles away."

After a while there was a quiet patch, and Maggie leaned back against the counter, and surveyed me. "So. How come someone like you is content just to serve up coffee on a Saturday night then, ay?"

"Someone like me?"

"Well you're not exactly hideous are you? That's why you got the job so quick. Come on. Tell us."

I laughed, shook my head, half turned away – and then I told her. It was such a relief, telling this stranger, telling it straight, no need to censor anything. I said I had this girlfriend who was determined to fix me up with a bloke, any bloke, to get me over this guy I'd been with, and just the thought made me sick, so I'd got the job to hide behind. And anyway I'd wanted something to occupy me because I was still obsessing over my ex, so much I thought I was going mad.

Maggie smiled at me as I burbled on, putting in the odd comment or enquiry, and I felt such warmth from her, and such a total lack of judgement, I just about spilled everything. All about how amazing Art had been, his energy and his looks and his evil sense of humour, and how much I'd want him, all the time, and how scared I was of never feeling that much again. Most girls, when you tell them about your love life, are comparing, measuring, matching themselves up to it, somehow. But she was just listening, with her weird green eyes fixed on mine. I've never opened up to anyone so soon after meeting them in my life.

"You think about wanting him back?" she said, when I finally came to a stop.

"Yes – all the time – but in a way I don't want to. What I want is to get *over* him. I mean – he wasn't perfect. He was pretty screwed up – we had some awful times. Sometimes I think he wasn't really right for me at all. It's just he was—"

"A magician. With a magic wand."

I frowned, then I realized what she meant, and I started to laugh. "It's not such a mystery, Coll," she gurgled. "How'd we get the world peopled without it? You know what's wrong with you, don't you. You're addicted. Not your fault."

I could have hugged her for saying that – not my

fault. For the last few months I'd felt as though it was all my fault – my fault for being weak.

"And now it's – what d'you call it, cold turkey time," she went on. "Coming off the addiction. Not pleasant. But I don't think your friend's right – I don't think you can snap out of it or whatever. It's like a wound – it's got to heal. You have to give it time."

"I've had time."

"Oh, what *rule book* says it has to all be dead and buried by the end of six months, ay? You know – we had this SE teacher at school we all used to take the piss out of. She used to bang on about sex needing to be in a *loving-stable-committed-context.* You know – like you needed to be married or living together at least. And we thought what an old prude she was, how safe, how boring. We used to shout it through the bedroom doors at parties – 'Hey – are you doing that in a loving-stable-committed-context?' Yeah, well, a lot of my friends were real slappers. Anyway, once I'd left school, and seen a bit more, I realized that that teacher wasn't trying to hold us back, you know? She was trying to, I don't know, *warn* us."

"Warn you off?"

"No – *no* – well, not in the sense of trying to get us to stay pure or anything. Just – warn us how out of depth we could get. Warn us we could get our hearts broken." She looked straight at me. "Like you've done."

There was a silence. You know those conversations you have when someone says something you've been beginning to get to yourself, and it's like this jump in understanding? That's how I felt then. I could feel this trembling, deep inside me, of excitement almost, the excitement you feel when you're both on the same wavelength, a new wavelength, one you haven't touched before.

"The thing is. . ." I began, tentatively, "it's really scary feeling like this. I mean – some days I think I'm seriously depressed, like I'll never drag myself out of it. And when all you get from other people is – God, yes, you *are* weird to still be unhappy over that loser, how long is it now, you should be over it – it just – it makes you feel worse."

"Yeah. It's like you're a failure, letting the side down, letting love be too important."

"That's it. That's it exactly. I'm letting the side down."

Maggie started to laugh. "Like it was a hockey match!"

"I know. But there's real impatience, and *disgust*, almost, from everyone, and in a way I can see their point – it's like – if you're a proper rounded person, you can take it in your stride."

"I think. . ." Maggie said slowly, "I think there's a power in it people won't admit to. I dunno – maybe the people who haven't felt it get irritated with people who have."

"Maybe," I said doubtfully.

"Anyway, it takes time. You're – you're *temporarily incapacitated*, OK? And that's OK, because you're getting there. And you should listen to yourself, what *you* want, how much time you need. Not other people. How do they know?"

There was a silence, and Maggie turned and started wiping down the counter. I looked at her and felt as though a weight had rolled off me. Maybe I wasn't a complete sad psycho after all. Maybe I *was* getting there.

"You sound like you know what you're talking about," I said. "Like you've been there too."

"Yeah, maybe," she said, offhand, and she turned away and started stacking cups, and I thought I wasn't going to hear about what she'd been through, not that night. Then she turned back to face me and said, "Yeah, I have. And it just about did my head in, like it's done yours. And now I'm steering clear."

"Oh," I said. "Right."

"When I say clear, I mean – I still go out, have a laugh, and if I fancy someone, I'll go for him and I'll have a good time. But I don't let stuff develop. I find it all claustrophobic, all this love stuff. And all the game playing and the power balances and shit – I've had a basin-full. I hate it."

"Oh," I said again. "Right."

"I'm not saying I won't ever get involved with a

guy again. Just – not for a while. A long while."

There was a pause, and I was about to ask her about this relationship she'd had, when she said: "Guys work two ways. They keep you on edge and doubtful – like your Art did – always hungry for more – or they saturate you, won't leave you alone. I've got a friend who's going out with a real saturation merchant at the moment. It sends me up the wall just being around them. He's always – *mauling* her. I was there last week and she was doing the washing up and he kept sliming up to her and putting his arms round her – she had rubber gloves on and a little dish mop. . ."

"Some people find them really sexy," I said. "Rubber gloves. Apparently."

"Well, this wasn't. It's like – mixing sex and domestic chores. It's yeuch."

"Yeah," I agreed. "And – you know – patronizing. How would *they* like it if they were up a ladder painting or something and you started groping *them*?"

We both paused for a moment, imagining it. Then Maggie started to growl with laughter. "They'd *love* it!" she gasped. "They'd just stand there with their paintbrush and *love* it!"

And we burst out laughing, like you do when the conversation has been intense and then somebody says something funny. We were still laughing when the door swung open and a voice said, "Glad to hear you so happy for once." I spun round and faced Val, and I felt this weird feeling – guilty, almost.

"Hi!" I said, sounding as pleased as I could manage. "You made it."

"Yes. We only saw a film." She laid bitter emphasis on the last word. "It was crap."

"No, it wasn't," said Greg, tiredly. "You just couldn't be bothered to work out what was going on in the early bits."

"I don't go to the cinema to *work*," Val snapped.

"Val, Greg, this is Maggie," I said hastily. "Maggie, this is—"

"Val and Greg," Maggie said. "Hi. Nice to meet you. You want a coffee?"

"How much is it?" asked Val. "These tarted up places always—"

"On the house," said Maggie.

"Great," said Greg. "Thank you."

Maggie turned away to get the coffee, and Val and I looked at each other over the counter. "So how's it going?" she asked.

"Good," I said. "Fine. Lots of tips." I wanted Val to be in no doubt I was only here for the money.

"I still think you're mad, giving up your Saturday nights," grumbled Val. "When're you going to have any *fun*." Fun, in Val's mouth, was beginning to sound like the grimmest duty going.

"She's had fun," said Greg. "She was having fun when we got here."

"Oh, so she was," said Val, nastily. "A darn sight more than I've had this evening. Maybe I should go and get a job too."

"Oh, for *Christ's* sake Val, you *chose* that film—"

"I didn't want to see a bloody film in the first place, remember?" she snarled. "I wanted to go out with—"

"Drop it," said Greg. "Please."

There was a potentially explosive pause, and then Maggie put the coffees on the counter, and we were able to let bleak small talk take over. Greg said he liked the colour of the café walls; Val said she'd once owned a plant like the one in the corner only much smaller. I willed the coffees to cool fast so they could drink up and leave.

"Well, we'd better be going," said Greg at last. "Finished, Val?"

"Yeah." She put down her cup. "See you Monday, Coll."

They both said thank you and walked to the door. Greg went to put his arm round Val, then seemed to think better of it, and they drifted out separately.

"Phew," said Maggie. "Young love. Who needs it."

"They're going through a bad patch," I said, loyally, repeating what I'd been told. "They used to be great together."

"That's kind of hard to believe, Coll. She's like seething with unhappiness. She needs help." I turned and gawped at her. *Val* needed help?

"God – *monogamy*," Maggie went on. "Who invented it? It's not natural. A couple of corpses chained together, slowly rotting. . ."

"Oh, Jesus, *Maggie*!"

"Well. I seriously don't think it works. To have kids maybe – not otherwise."

"OK – what does work?"

She laughed. "I dunno. I'm still working on that one."

"Well, let me know when you've sorted it out," I said. "I want to know."

It was nearly eleven and the last customers were straggling out. Maggie showed me the shutting-up-shop routine, then said she'd hang on for Bill, but I should go.

I felt really tired, but good tired. I had my hand on the door when I remembered something and turned back. "Maggie, you know Bill said I was on, like, a trial? Well if I don't wait for him, what will—"

"Oh, I'll tell him you've passed," she answered. "The other trial runners weren't a patch on you, even if you are the sad, suffering victim type. Hey, Coll, your face! I was only joking."

"You better be," I said. "See you next week."

* * *

47

Three weeks later, and the importance of my Saturday night job had grown out of all proportion. It was just about the best thing in my life. I liked the work; it was busy and cheerful, it made me feel capable and confident and I didn't have to put on any kind of an act, doing it. I felt better and I slept better afterwards. And when the week at school began to get me down – I had Saturday night to look forward to again. It was like – I don't know, I'd been locked into an old shed, all stale and dusty, and someone had wrenched off a bit of panel, and at last a bit of light was coming through. I wasn't free yet, but I could see the outside, and I could breathe a bit more easily.

Maggie was the biggest reason I enjoyed it so much. She had this tough attitude to life, as though you had to get it by the balls before it got you, that was somehow very cheering to be alongside. And yet at the same time she was a brilliant listener, and boy, was it good just to be able to burble everything out. Not to have to try and pretend I wasn't feeling what I was feeling. In between the wiping down and the clearing up, I went over everything: the longing, the dreams, the fits of crying, and she'd just listen; as if nothing could faze her. There was something so strong inside her. I'd tell her I owed her therapist money, and she'd just grin and make some joke and we'd both end up in fits of laughter.

She was great at boosting your confidence, too. Generous with compliments, and with a kind of understanding about who you were. I began to feel good about myself again. Every now and then she'd come out with these gems, like some kind of oracle. "Who told you you had to be strong all the time?" she said once. "You're too scared of cracking up, Coll. You'll get through this. And what you felt for him – it's opened you up. Some people never get that open. Maybe you should be glad."

This was the first time I'd heard anyone say anything positive about a guy leaving you feeling like a crushed worm. Val and everyone talked as though what I was feeling made me smaller; Maggie talked as though it might actually be growth. I knew she was speaking from experience and I'd try to get her to tell me about what had happened to her, but she wouldn't be drawn on it. She just repeated that she was steering well clear of "love stuff" for the moment, and then she'd pull a stupid face and cross her fingers to ward off vampires and that would be that.

She asked me to bring in a photo of Art to show her, and I did, one of the ones I'd taken on that holiday we'd had in Greece, right before we split up. He looked completely gorgeous in it. Just a pair of shorts and bare brown skin and his hair all spiky from the sea salt drying on it, and he had this funny, yobby expression, because he was halfway through saying if I took any more photos of him he was going to lob the camera over the cliffs.

It had taken me ages to be able to look at that photo and be able to stand what I felt when I did. Maggie took it from me, and laughed. "H'm. Yeah. I wouldn't kick him out of bed."

I sighed. "He just – oh God. He was *perfect*."

"Apart from being an immature selfish screwed-up headcase."

"Yeah. Apart from that. But he had potential, Maggie he was changing, I swear he was—"

"Until he ran off, yeah. And you're getting over him. Day by day, in every way, it's getting less. Come on, Coll – repeat it!"

I laughed, and went off to do the washing up with a really light heart. The feeling of being divided against myself, the feeling of being eaten up inside, was getting less. Somehow, now I'd accepted just how smashed up I'd been, I was beginning to heal.

I felt more relaxed at school; Val and I reached a kind of equilibrium, nothing like the old days, but comfortable enough. And I was more open at home. Mum and I even had one of our old rows about me not helping enough to get the supper ready. It was almost fun in a nostalgic kind of a way.

And then, one morning, there was a letter for me.

Chapter nine

It was lying on the mat like a promise, like a knife, like a detonator. I didn't need to see the New Zealand postmark or check the writing, all smeared black ink, to know it was from Art. I picked it up, went back upstairs, pulled down the flight of steps to my attic and climbed up them, pulling them back up behind me. In one section of my head something was saying "You'll be really late for school" but that was dim and far away, completely unimportant. I was like an animal going back to its den, back to safety, only I wasn't running away from something that was going to tear me apart – I was taking it with me.

Dear Coll,

I'm drunk and I don't know why I'm writing this now. I think about you a lot and what you said when we split up and I still can't work it out. Some nights here I've felt so screwed up the only thing I could do was drink myself to sleep.

Anyway, the money's running out faster than I can earn it, and I need to get back, get myself together, get to college in the autumn. It's been great here but I don't want the dropout life for ever. I'll stay with the old man when I get back. I'd like to see you but I'll understand if you don't want to see me. A lot of stuff has been happening to me, and you are the only person I could really talk to, you were a real friend.

Love, Art

I sat back on my bed, heart hammering. So that's what I was. A friend. You weren't my friend, Art. You were my lover. My first lover, my only lover. Friends make you laugh and support you and stop you feeling alone. They don't make you go to bed night after night curled up in misery. They can't make you full of ecstasy one minute and full of despair the next. They don't have such power over you, for good or bad. You're not my friend.

I scanned the letter for hidden meanings, betrayals of intense love, signs of regret, hints of intention. I rolled every word around my mouth, sucked it dry of its meaning, couldn't come to any conclusions. Except for the fact that he wanted to see me. Except for the fact that he'd said I was the only person he could really talk to, when once I'd despaired of ever getting him to open up. Then I burst into tears, not even sure what the tears meant, hid the letter at the bottom of my desk drawer, and went off to school half an hour late. I didn't tell anyone there it had arrived, least of all Val. I knew she'd tell me to bin it or burn it.

That night as soon as I got home I got Art's letter out and reread it, then I read it again and again, I couldn't put it down. I didn't know what to think about it, how to get a handle on it. I knew I had to do something or I'd combust, so I left the house and headed down town to the café to see Maggie.

"Hi, Coll!" she said, surprised, as I walked in. Then she took in my expression. "What's up?"

"Can we talk?" I muttered.

Maggie turned round and checked the clock on the wall. "We close early tonight," she said. "About twenty minutes' time. Want to wait for me?"

"I'll come back," I said. "If that's OK."

"Sure it's OK. We can wander into the centre and you can buy me some chips."

I smiled at her, really gratefully, and left. Then I sleep-walked through the shops with Art's letter in my bag and going round and round in my head until it was time to go back and meet her.

I handed her the letter as soon as we'd made it out of the door, and she scanned it and said, "Selfish shit."

"Yeah?"

"Yeah. It's all about him and what he's going through and what *he* needs. He must *know* what effect this letter will have on you – just arriving, out of the blue – but he doesn't say anything about *that*."

"Yeah, but what could he say? 'Hey, I know this will be a thunderbolt to your heart, kid, but –'"

Maggie laughed. "Like it, Coll. You want to take up writing bad lyrics for ballads."

"Well, it *is* a thunderbolt. I was just beginning to feel better, you know walking forward – and now this letter comes – and I feel I'm just back into waiting and wondering and *hoping* and—"

"So you wish it hadn't come."

I sort of collapsed then, back against the café window. "No. I don't. I can't. I *want* to see him. I really want to see him. It's just – it's like it's wiped everything else *out*. Nothing's important beside it. That feels . . . *awful.* And now I'll be all screwed up waiting to hear from him and I just – I just don't feel I have any *say* in it, that's what's so horrible. It's like – he's got all the power."

"Only because you give it to him," Maggie murmured.

"*No.*" I was close to tears. "No, Maggie, that's just not true. I can't help it. I don't have a choice."

"Oh, Coll that is just so – you *do* have a choice. It's your decision whether you see him or not, for a start. You could *decide* just to tear the letter up!"

"Yeah, I could. But I can't decide what my head's full of, can I? It would be – crazy not to see him. Dishonest."

"*Dishonest? Why* the *hell* – Look, Coll, remember when I said you were addicted to him – and you agreed? You meet him again – isn't that like just going back on the stuff again? Isn't it just stirring it all up?"

I looked at her hopelessly. "I don't know."

"You want to see him – because you hope it'll work out this time. You hope he'll grab hold of you and tell you he'll slit his throat if you won't be his."

I laughed. "Some hope."

There was a long silence. Then she said, "Yeah, OK, you're right. You do have to see him. You don't know what's been happening to him, and he's written, and – unfinished business."

"It is," I said, eagerly, gratefully. "It is unfinished. We broke up really badly. I hope – I hope he's been doing some thinking, I hope that stuff he wrote about being screwed up is because he was screwed up by us. Like I was. I think that's what I want. Even if it can't work out for us, I want to know I *meant* something to him."

"You don't have to meet him to know that. You can tell that from the letter."

I was silent. Maggie sighed and linked her arm through mine, and we started walking into the town together. "What did you say when you split up?" she asked.

"What?"

"In the letter he says he thinks all the time about what you said when you split up."

"Oh. Right. That's when I told him I was in love with him, couldn't live without him – you know, stuff guaranteed to make the average guy pack his bags straight away and head for New Zealand."

"Right. And now he's coming back. You know – if he *doesn't* want you back – he's being really cruel, getting in touch again. I mean, he knows how you feel."

"Yeah, but – he won't think that way, Maggie. It was *six months* ago. He'll think I'm over him. He'll have had dozens of girlfriends since, and he'll think even I've managed one or two."

"One or two what?"

"Boyfriends, idiot."

She laughed, and I sighed. "I dunno," I went on. "I've got to do this, I've got to see him again, but it feels awful. Terrifying. Like I'm stepping off the ledge again – laying myself open to get really hurt again. Shit, it feels awful."

"So remind me again why you have to see him?"

I groaned, and Maggie said, "No, OK. I understand. Hey – maybe it'll be OK. Maybe it'll be a huge anti-climax and you'll think – who is this sad self-obsessed git, and why was I so gone on him?"

Then she squeezed my arm, and we wandered on together.

Chapter ten

The next few days, I made myself so busy I didn't get time to think. I pile-drived into two late essays; I cleaned my room out; and I swam, twice. By Saturday morning I was feeling pretty shattered, but I still woke up early, with a weird feeling of panic in the pit of my stomach. I crawled to the end of the bed and sat wrapped in my duvet, thinking how I could fill up the hours until I went to work in the café.

I heard Mum get up and stomp downstairs to fill the kettle; then I heard the phone ring once, and my little sister Sarah run up to answer it in Mum's room. Sarah had just got to that stage where she had a Social Life; and I'd given up racing her for the phone, because it was usually for her. Her social life was a lot more active than mine, if you want to know the truth.

I sat there, rocking myself slightly, half listening to her, and then something about the lack of giggles, something about the sharp tone of her voice, made me shoot over to the attic hatch and hang down like a bat to listen.

"Yes, but who shall I say's *calling*?" she was insisting shrilly. Then – "Why *should* I just get her if I don't know who you *are*?"

I slithered down the steps and went into Mum's room. "Is that for me?" I hissed, and already my heart was pounding like a road drill, and my legs were like jelly. I don't know how I made it across the room.

"Yes," bleated Sarah, "but he won't say who he is and I think it's – *you know*!" She held out the phone towards me – she looked almost scared.

I took it and jerked my head towards the door, and she went immediately, even shutting the door after her. Then I put the phone to my ear and whispered, "Hello."

"Hi, Coll. It's me."

Me. After six months' silence, just "me". And the thing is, it would have been completely phoney to have said more.

"Yeah. Hi."

"I thought Sarah was going to put the phone down on me then."

"Yeah, well –"

"At least your mum didn't answer."

"Um."

"Coll – did you get my letter?"

"Yes."

"I was pretty drunk when I wrote it."

"Oh," I gulped. "Are you – where are you?

"Kilburn. Dad's flat."

Kilburn. A short train ride away. My blood was

pounding so hard now I could hear it in my ears, it was like I was going to pass out.

"So – you going to see me, or not?" he said.

"Er – I dunno," I answered, knowing I would, knowing I had to.

"I thought we could maybe meet halfway. No big deal. Just to meet. Yeah?"

"Yeah. OK."

"Tonight?"

"No." I said it without thinking, and then I was glad I had said no. I needed one more evening before I faced this. I needed Maggie. "I'm busy."

"OK. Tomorrow?

"Yeah, OK. The afternoon'd be best for me." I didn't want to meet him at night.

"Great. Covent Garden's one change for you, right? Can we meet there?"

"Sure."

"Let's meet at that café – you know, Franks."

"OK, then."

"Three-ish?"

"OK."

"Great. See you then."

I croaked "Bye" and put the phone down, and then I sat back on Mum's bed, and waited to see what would happen with my emotions and my mind, like when you cut yourself badly and part of you just stands back and ogles at the blood.

When I feel desire, I usually feel it in this long slow spread, all the way up through my legs and my groin into my stomach, but the minute I'd heard his voice, I'd felt it, full force, slam, everywhere all at once, as though a power switch had been thrown. And it was still there now, burning. At the same time I felt devastated, destroyed, throat closed up with tears. No big deal, he'd said – no big deal. And my brain was screaming out "Fuck off, Art. Who the hell d'you think you *are*?"

It was amazing I didn't just blow up there and then, with the stuff that was slogging it out inside me. *Breathe*, I told myself, like some yoga videotape. *Breathe. Focus. You don't have to do anything you don't want to do. It's your choice. You're in charge.* You *decide.*

It was comical, really. I felt about as in charge as a hedgehog about to be hit by a truck. But I chanted this refrain off and on throughout the day and, somehow, it helped. *Hang on to yourself,* I told myself. *You're used to feeling pole-axed by this guy, and surviving. It's over – you can't get hurt any more. You're going to go and meet Art but you can back out, come home, put a stop to it any time. Just keep breathing. Feel your feet on the ground.*

And it was weird, as I headed off to work that night I realized I did feel a bit calmer, more in charge. It was like acceptance. Fate.

Maggie didn't have anything new to say when I told her; she just rolled her eyes and wished me luck. I felt as though everything was on hold until tomorrow.

Chapter eleven

I made sure I looked really good when I set off the next afternoon, as good as I could manage. Shiny hair, new jeans, great-coloured jumper. I sat on the tube feeling sick with nerves, and as I travelled, I tried to create this calm, protective shell round about myself. I visualized it there; sealed, impenetrable. Whatever happened, whatever was going on inside me, I was somehow going to keep it contained, I wasn't going to show a thing. *You had to come*, I told myself, *you had to find out. And now you don't know what's going to happen, but however lacerated you feel you can get through this, you can walk away.*

It was harder dealing with the hope. I wouldn't let myself acknowledge it fully but I knew it was there inside me, fluttering, tearful, reaching out its arms.

I walked out of the station and up to the café like a zombie. I saw Art as soon as I'd opened the door, sitting at a window table across the room. Some sixth sense made him look up as I came through the door, and he waved, wide-eyed, unsmiling.

I clamped down on my reaction to seeing him after all this time before I could be sure what my reaction was. Then I put all my effort into walking towards him. It took me thirty seconds to cross the room. Any little, tiny hope I'd had that he'd leap up from the table and wrap his arms around me and say "Coll, oh Coll, how could I have left you" withered completely in those thirty seconds.

But he did get to his feet. And he did put out a hand, as though to touch me, and he bent towards me, as if he might kiss me, but he didn't do either, he just gestured towards a chair, and I sat down. Then he asked me if I'd like a coffee, and I said yes. He called to the waitress and ordered two coffees while I made myself breathe slowly, through my nose, trying not to show that I was shaking.

Art propped his elbows on the table and said, "So. How you been?"

I didn't answer straight away. His face, that close, that perfect – it nearly did me in. Every part of it was so familiar. I'd kissed every inch of it, I'd touched every bit of it. I felt like it was mine.

I shrugged, "Oh, you know. Working."

"Oh, right. Exams, yeah?"

"Not long to go now."

"You'll sail through. Brainbox."

That babyish word – it was too affectionate. Suddenly I couldn't look at his face any longer, so I made the big mistake of glancing down at the table, where my eyes fell on his hand. Browner than I remembered it, but I knew it, every bit of it. And it knew me. How I stopped myself reaching out to get hold of it, I don't know.

"How was New Zealand?" I croaked, idiotically.

"Oh – great. It's an amazing place, Coll. It's so . . . it's so *open*. Not just the landscape, the people too. Not like here. Everyone's relaxed, there." He laughed. "The dope helps."

"What sort of work did you do?" I went on, neutrally, safely. "Where did you stay?"

"Well, when I got there, I was like – shit scared. What I'd done – just dropping out and clearing off like that – it hit me, boom. And then I got worried about just surviving. I didn't know anyone there – no one knew me. . . But I had enough cash on me for this sort of hostel place – they gave me the address at the tourist office at the airport – and when I got there it was full of a load of people who didn't seem to know what they were doing either, but it was like – it didn't matter. That made me feel better. I took a couple of days just to chill, just to – I slept a lot."

He paused, and we both looked down at the table between us. I wanted to ask him what had made him just up stakes and go, what had finally cracked in him just a few weeks into a new term, but that question was too close to the whole thing of us splitting up.

"The second day, I met these three great guys – American. Couple of years older than me. Working their way round the world. I felt like a real idiot, next to them – like I didn't know anything. But we got on great, and when they moved on, they asked me to go with them. They wanted to spend some time in New Zealand – they wanted a break, to get some surfing in. Also they were broke. All four of us got a job on a sheep farm straight away, shifting stuff, clearing up – we demolished this barn – it was really hard work for a fortnight, then we got paid, *well*, and we took off for the beach. That was just – that was *amazing*, Coll. You worked your arse off, then you just stopped. With all this amazing beauty round you. When you were hungry you ate, you slept when you wanted to. Right there on the sand. And you'd sit at night, at sunset, and watch this great ball of fire just drop into the sea."

"Wow," I said, inadequately.

"The beaches are fantastic, Coll. And the sea – it's so clear. The snorkelling – you should just see the colours out there – reds, blues, purple – the fish are like something from another planet. They're blinding." He looked up at me, smiling, reliving it. "God I miss it. It's so grey here. Even the plants – even the green is grey, here."

My eyes were fixed on his eyes as he talked; I was putting all my effort into appearing calm. His voice was the same as it had always been. I could feel it echoing inside me.

Art drained his cup of coffee and announced, "I learned to surf, Coll. I bought a board."

"Yeah? You any good?"

"So so. It's weird, it's not about skill, like rugby and stuff. It's all about letting go – giving yourself up to something bigger, you know? You're not pitting yourself against the waves – you're going with them. Being part of them. You battle the sea, you're lost. It's only when you let go that it – really happens for you." He grinned at me. "Bit like sex."

I felt myself going scarlet. What was he playing at, dropping sex in the conversation like that?

"You score some dope, then you score some waves . . . it was just incredible. Nature is the truth there, you know? The teacher. It's just so . . . so *total*. It's . . . you just get into a rhythm with it, and that's it, that's your life. . ."

This new, cosmic side to Art was beginning to faze me. I half liked it, because it was so open, and I half hated it, because it was part of the life he'd had since we'd split up and there was absolutely no mention of me in it. "So how d'your dad take it," I said, dampeningly. "You just turning up again."

Art seemed to deflate. "Not good. I can't afford not to stay with him right now, though. I s'pose we reached some kind of truce. He's massively annoyed with me, but the other night I heard him on the phone to someone, and he was like – almost bragging about what I'd done. Well, if he thinks it was good, he should say so to my face. Dishonest bastard. He won't ever be straight about anything. So now I'm eating his food and taking his money and I don't give a shit."

"But you've got months to go before the new term at college. The whole summer."

"Yeah. First I've got to get a place somewhere else. I'm not going back to that poxy business studies course. Then I'll get a job of some sort. Then maybe I'll go away again. Maybe Turkey. Then I'll go back to college, and this time I'll stick it out."

And until next term, I thought, *you're going to be in Kilburn. One change on the tube.* "I'm going to take a year off," I announced.

"You should, Coll. You really should. It's amazing, just being able to travel, no time restraints."

"So – how long did you stay at the beach? With those three guys?"

"Well, after about six weeks I'd got a bit fed up with just dossing. I'd got friendly with the guy who owned the big beach bar, and one day he offered me a job. Place to sleep, too – hot showers. Soon after, the guys started talking about moving on, farm working again, but I told them I didn't want to go along with them. I'd really got into surfing, and the bar job was too good. Great fun, good food, and people tipped really well. Especially the women."

He smirked at me, and I refused to smile back. "I really stacked up some money over the next couple of months, and I got a lot better at surfing. Then after that I took two months off and just travelled."

"On your own?" I said.

"Yeah." He paused, then added, "At first."

I wasn't going to ask who he was with. It was quite possibly female, and I didn't want to know that. Not yet.

"It was weird, saying goodbye to those three blokes," he went on. "I mean – we'd been in each others' company twenty-four hours a day for weeks on end, we'd got really close – one of them, Mac, he just about saved my life once, when I got wiped."

"Wiped?"

"A big wave. The sea kept working me, but he pulled me out."

"So have you got their addresses or something?"

"Nah. No point."

"God. That's a bit cold, isn't it?"

Art shrugged. "We had what we had – we knew no one was going to start sending Christmas cards. We just said goodbye. It was . . . honest."

I suddenly felt incredibly tired, strung out with nerves.

What, I thought, *am I doing here, discussing his travels like I'm nothing more than an old friend, an acquaintance?* I couldn't bear it. I couldn't bear the disappointment or the pleasure of sitting close to him, the shock of it, and the effort of holding myself together. Any minute now I was going to throw myself at him and start howling.

I made myself go through the charade of checking my watch. "I should go," I announced. "I'm going out tonight."

"Yeah?" he said. "Who with?"

"Oh, just. . ."

"Got someone new?"

I toyed briefly with the idea of inventing a fabulous new boyfriend for myself. "Just friends," I said.

"But have you?"

"What?"

"Got someone new?"

"No. What about you?"

"Oh, nothing I haven't left behind."

Like you left me behind, I thought. And I stood up to get out of the café before he could tell me any details, before I heard myself asking for details, because already I could feel myself being eaten up by jealousy and curiosity.

Art stood up too, and in ill-fitting silence we paid the bill, left the café and walked along to the station together. We stood in the entrance, people jostling us as they pushed past to catch their trains. "My platform's that way," I said, pointing.

"Yeah, I know."

"OK, well –"

"Can I call you again?"

Pleasure flooded into me, treacherous pleasure. There was a pause. Then I made myself say "Why?"

"Oh, I dunno. You're just – you're good to talk to, Coll. Look, no hassle. I know you're working hard right now."

He half turned away, and I heard myself saying, "Yeah, look – phone me, and we'll see, OK?"

"OK," he said, then he put his left hand on my right shoulder, and bent towards me, and kissed me on the cheek.

I wasn't prepared for the shock of that impact again, after all that time. I wasn't prepared for the closeness, the scent of him. "I have to go," I choked out. Then I turned and ran, clattering down the concrete stairs, half hearing him shout "See you!"

My train arrived almost immediately and I clambered on to it gratefully. I found an empty set of four seats at the end and made myself as small as I could in the corner. Then I slowly, carefully, raised up the gate that I'd kept clanged shut on everything I'd been feeling over the last few hours, and let it all out. I let all the hope and ecstasy and anguish of seeing him again come flooding out and fill me. I went over everything Art had said, every look he'd given me. I admitted it all. The ways he'd changed, the ways he'd stayed the same – the way he'd lit up when he'd been talking about the beach life, the surfing. The way he'd said surfing was like sex. Water, the sea, swimming, we'd talked about sex like that sometimes. I'd told him once that my orgasm was like waves, and he'd said he'd felt it like waves too.

And then I made myself face that he hadn't asked me to go back with him. I made myself admit that I'd wanted that, badly. I wanted him. I wanted him with every atom in me, and that scared me senseless, while at the same time part of me was glad that I could feel that much. Part of me felt so alive, just to feel it – more alive than I'd felt in months.

I sat there, watching the trees and the houses whizz past the train windows, half crying, half smiling, not knowing what I was going to do, what I *could* do, and something my gran once said to me came into my head. It was just after Granddad had died, and she said one of the worst bits was wanting Granddad to comfort her about it. At the time I'd laughed, embarrassed, not really understanding – I mean, he was dead, how *could* he comfort her? But now I understood. Just before I'd left the café I'd felt so overwhelmed with everything I'd wanted to burst into tears right there and tell Art how fabulous it was, meeting up with him again, but how awful it was too, how much it screwed me up, not being lovers any more, making stupid conversation. Art wasn't much good at talking but he could have put his arms round me and kissed my hair and said, "Hey, shut up Coll. You're OK. It'll work out."

I couldn't, any more than my gran could talk to my granddad, but that's what I wanted most of all.

Chapter twelve

I didn't speak to anyone about seeing Art over the next few days. Partly because he was taboo, with Mum, with Val, with everyone, but mainly because I was completely absorbed in all the feelings that had been stirred up in me again.

Then, on Wednesday night, about half past nine in the evening, the phone rang. Mum answered it, and held the receiver out to me with her mouth twisted into the type of disapproval that meant there was a male on the other end of it.

"*Joe* somebody," she said, heavily.

Joe. Art's ex best friend. The only person I knew who really knew Art. My heart started thudding. I hadn't spoken to him since just before Christmas, since I'd bumped into him at the shopping centre and he'd told me about Art doing a runner to New Zealand.

I took the phone. "Joe? Hi! How are you?"

"I'm fine. Back for the Easter break."

"You're joking. We've got weeks to go before our term ends.

"Yeah, well, when you're a responsible student like me, you get trusted with longer holidays. . ."

"Yeah, yeah. Seriously, how's it going?"

"Great. Better, anyway. I've met some really good people. Not doing enough work though. I've got three essays to finish off these holidays and about a million books to read."

"Aw. Well, don't expect sympathy from me. I feel like I'm on a nuclear countdown already."

"Oh, God, yes. Awful. I can just dimly remember the terror of walking into the exam hall – I mean, the exams themselves I've blocked out, *whoa*, *serious* nightmare material, I still wake up sweating and screaming and—"

"Joe –"

"Yeah?"

"Shut up, will you?"

"OK. You all right apart from that?"

"Yes, I'm fine."

"That's great. Um . . . Coll. . ."

"Yeah?"

"I saw Art yesterday. He's – er – he's back."

"Oh. Right."

"I didn't know whether to let you know or not – I mean, you probably couldn't care less by now, but I said I'd phone you if I heard anything about him and –"

"So how was he?"

"OK. Bit hippy. Wanking on about the glories of surfing. Think he got into dope in a big way out there.

He looked OK – tanned, fitter than he was. Actually, he looked great, the bastard."

"And did he tell you he saw me, Sunday?"

There was an explosive pause. "He – *saw* you."

"Yeah. He wrote, then he phoned, then we met, Sunday."

"No. No, he didn't tell me, or I wouldn't've phoned you, would I? I dunno, he – what's he playing at? Why didn't he tell me?"

"Well – maybe I just didn't come up. In the conversation."

"Oh, you came up all right, Coll."

"Yeah – what? Come on Joe – what?"

"Are you two guys getting back together now, or what?"

"No – *no*! We just met for a coffee – it was weird – like you said, he went on about surfing and –"

"I don't get him. Why didn't he tell me he'd just seen you."

"What was he saying about me, Joe? *Please*."

"D'you want to get back with him?"

"*Joe!*"

"OK, OK. Just stuff about – it being scary letting women in too close. That kind of thing. Getting his head back together again. I mean – I told you before, I'm sure you were one of the reasons he took off to New Zealand in the first place."

"So – was he like . . . was he saying. . .?" I paused,

gasped. I realized I hadn't breathed for ages. "Was he saying he was over me now?"

"Well . . . yes. Kind of."

I gripped the receiver, told myself I was OK.

"He said he was a lot more sorted out," Joe went on. "Avoiding getting – screwed up and stuff. That's why it doesn't make any sense, him calling you up and arranging to see you."

"I suppose he just wants us to be friends. Maybe."

"Well the way he was talking, friendship wasn't really a . . . well, a. . ."

"A *what*?"

"What do you want, Coll? Are you over him?"

Joe sounded so kind when he said that I could feel my throat growing thick with tears, and I didn't dare speak.

"Coll? You still there? Coll?"

"Joe . . . could we . . . could you bear it if I . . . would you meet me for a drink or something?"

Joe and I arranged to meet that Friday night, in a pub on the outskirts of town. I felt in some uneasy way that I was using Joe, that it wasn't quite fair, what I was doing, but I shook those thoughts off.

He was already there when I arrived, looking the same as ever. Floppy hair, badly fitting jacket. Kind eyes.

"So, tell me about university life," I said, as soon as

we'd got a drink and sat down. Obsessional I might be, but I still had a few good manners left.

"Well – it's great," Joe said. "But . . . you know . . . overwhelming. I feel like I'm running up a down escalator half the time. There's just so much to keep up with. Friends, work, living—"

"Laundry."

"That was one of the first things to go. Then washing. No, don't get up, I'm joking. It's just – it's harder than I thought it would be, Coll. You meet a bunch of exciting people and it's all great and then you realize you're weeks behind on your course. So you head for the library and get your head down and then you realize you're becoming a real saddo who never goes out."

"Can't you like – *integrate* it more?"

"That's just what my personal tutor says. It's all about balancing, she says, and juggling."

"Sounds like a bad circus act."

"It feels like it sometimes." He sat back in his chair, closed his eyes, and smiled. "I dunno, I still wish I'd had a year off. I feel like a complete kid there, sometimes. I mean – I've only left home for holidays, up to now. And just about everyone I meet seems to have done some amazing gap year. The *women* – they petrify me."

"Oh, come on, Joe –"

"They do. I still have boys' school syndrome. I

can't deal with them. Well, I'm OK when I've had a few beers, but in a tutorial or something, I'm hopeless. I don't understand how you can have a discussion about something with girls there and not think about which one of them you want to get off with."

I laughed. "Can't you do both at the same time?"

"Well – sometimes. There's this . . . *angel*, in our politics group. I swear I haven't dared say a thing in front of her. In case she thinks I'm a prat."

"What kind of stuff does she say?"

"Dunno. I don't really listen."

"Oh, great. You just ogle her?"

"No! Well – OK, yeah." There was a pause, then Joe said, "Come on, Coll. You didn't get me here to talk about who I fancy."

"Yes, I did. Partly."

"OK. Well – we've done that, *partly*. Now let's home in on Wonder Boy."

I could feel myself going red. "I just – look. Just tell me what he was saying about me. When you met."

"I've told you."

"No, you haven't. Not really."

Joe fixed me with a long look. "First I'd like to know how you stand. It might affect how I tell it."

"Oh, *Joe*! I don't know where I stand – that's the whole point! I'm – I'm totally messed up about him, still. I probably shouldn't've seen him again. I should've just told him no. I had this idea – I thought when we met we'd be able to talk like we did before. I thought we'd be able to discuss what we were feeling. . ."

Joe pulled a face. "I thought you couldn't do that even when you were going out together."

"Look – I just didn't think all the closeness would be gone. I mean – it's like a whole new set of ground rules, now. I couldn't ask him anything – anything real. We spent the whole time talking about the fish he'd seen."

"Whoa. Thrilling."

"Yeah. Anyway. I need you to – I just want you to tell me the truth. About what he said to you."

Joe sighed. "OK. But I don't think you'll like it. He was all 'Coll really screwed up my mind, but a few months surfing and travelling straightened me out'. He has this picture of himself, the lone survivor. I mean – you really got to him, Coll, when you were together, but he seemed to see it as a bit of a . . . well, a disease. Something he's better off without."

I looked down. "Great."

"Oh, come on, Coll, don't get upset. It's his problem, right? It's nothing against you. No one *normal* sees . . . sees *feeling* stuff as a disease. You got under his skin like no one else has done, and he can't let that happen in case he gets hurt."

I shrugged. "So why did he call me up?"

"That's what doesn't fit. He was talking like – like he'd got over you, like you were in the past. Like – once bitten, twice shy."

"Did he . . . did he tell you about getting involved with anyone else?"

The silence was just long enough for me to be sure that he had.

"Joe – tell me. I want to know. I want the *truth*."

"Oh, Coll. You know what a sleaze merchant he was before he met you. He's just reverting to type."

"How?" I said in a small voice.

"Oh, God. He did a lot of pulling when he was working at that beach bar. I don't think any of it lasted. I got fed up listening, if you want to know the truth. He seriously pisses me off. It half cripples me to even ask someone out for a drink, and he's out there shagging everything in sight. . . Oh, Coll, *sorry*." Joe leant across the table, got hold of my hand, and squeezed it apologetically. "Don't get upset. You're better off without him. Think of the diseases he might have picked up."

"So . . . it was all . . . it was all one night stands and stuff?"

There was another revealing pause. "Joe? Was it?"

"Well . . . there was Maria."

I could feel something venomous stirring inside me, next to all the hurt. "Maria?"

Joe sighed. "The original older woman. Some

divorcee, early thirties. Well off. She picked him up when he was hitch-hiking and they stayed together for the next month or something. Like some crap road movie."

"Month?" I whispered. "Where did they stay?"

"Well – she was travelling. Only *she* had a great car and *she* was staying in hotels. He told her he was twenty-three. She paid for everything. What a tart that guy is. No, what's the word? Gigolo. Gig-o-lo."

"Joe, your jealousy's *really* showing," I muttered, mechanically.

He gave me a long look. "So's yours."

I was staring at the table, trying not to see all the images that had rushed into my mind, unbidden. Art's profile in the passenger seat of some fast car, Art across a restaurant table smiling, showing all his teeth, Art lounging on some huge, pillow-strewn bed, Art in a shower while Maria, all sophistication and experience, handed him a towel.

I felt like I wanted to die.

Joe leaned forward and got hold of my hand again, and this time he hung on to it. "Don't let it eat you up, Coll. I mean – how corny can you get. She even bought clothes for him. Nauseating."

"Yeah," I sniffed. "Did she?"

"Yeah. Sickening. I bet they were really crap clothes, too. Gigolo clothes."

"Silk shirts," I gulped.

"Maroon boxers."

"Cashmere sweaters."

"*Yeah*. And I bet she called him by some sicky pet name, too. . ." He squeezed my fingers. "Come on, Coll, cheer up. You're worth – he's not worth it."

"I *know*," I wailed. "I know. I just wish – *he's* the disease, not me. He's like some kind of a virus, I swear he is. I think I'm over him and then . . . and then . . . it all comes back, just like, just like. . ."

"Flu."

"Yeah. Oh, God, it scares me sometimes. I think it'll take for ever."

"It won't. Come on, Coll, it's over. *Really* over. Think of him dogging round after all those women. What a lech. What a turn off."

"I know . . . I *know*! It's just – *seeing* him again was so . . . and you hear this stuff, how you never get over your first lover . . . how it's like some kind of an *imprint* in you. . ."

There was a long, hopeless sort of pause, then Joe let go of my hand and sat back, stretching a little, his hands behind his head. "So. You going to see him again?"

"I don't know. I don't *know*. He said he'd call me, but –"

"Only I should tell you he's going to be a lot nearer now. Nearer here, I mean."

I looked at Joe stupidly. "Nearer. . .?"

"I said he could stay at my place for a while. He said his dad was driving him psycho . . . we have two spare rooms now, both my sisters have left home . . . my mum said it would be all right. . ."

"Oh, terrific," I muttered, while I felt this great, scary, treacherous flood of excitement at the thought that Art would be so much nearer to me. I let this subside a little, then looked up and said, "Well, at least *you've* forgiven him, Joe."

"Yeah, well, that was two years ago. And I haven't got a girlfriend at the moment. No one he can pinch. And – you know, he needs help and a mate's a mate. Even someone like Art."

I smiled, then I said, "Did Art ever tell you you were the reason we split up?"

I wasn't at all prepared for the extraordinary expression that crossed Joe's features. Kind of amazement, mixed with pleasure.

"Seriously, you were. You know that time I called you up, right after Art and I'd got back from Greece – we met to talk, remember? You were great, you really—"

"Of course I remember."

"Well, he saw us in your car. Laughing together. So naturally, he thought we were having it off too. We had a big bust up over it and he ended up telling me he couldn't cope with what he was feeling and . . . blah, blah."

Joe let out a long breath. "No, he didn't tell me that. As far as I knew, he had no idea we'd even met up. Weird."

I shook my head. "He is such a closed book, that guy."

"Yeah. I don't s'pose even he knows what's going on."

Chapter thirteen

We left the pub soon after that and Joe said he'd walk me home because he could do with some air. So we wandered along, arm in arm, and laughed about him getting all tongue-tied with his angel in the politics group, and then about Art being the King of Sleaze and me being smitten with him even so, which was proof that I had no taste or dis-*cern*-ment as Joe called it.

It was so easy, talking with Joe. Much easier than it had ever been with Art, somehow. I guess because I didn't care so obsessively what Joe thought of me.

Joe said goodbye outside my gate, and I thanked him, then I reached up and kissed him on the cheek.

"Call me when you want to," he said. "Any time. And don't let it get to you."

"Thanks, Joe. Listen – I do Saturday nights at that new café, Perk Up – you know? In the centre of town. Any time you want a free cappuccino. . ."

"Right. I'll be there," Joe said, smiling, then he ducked and kissed me back.

I slept in late the next morning. By eleven, Mum was bellowing up the stairs that she needed bread from the shops if I wanted any lunch, so I went out and bought some, then I cleared up my room and got a bit of work out of the way. By the time I'd finished the history I needed to do it was time to start getting ready to go to the café.

As I was making up my eyes I realized how much I was looking forward to seeing Maggie again. I wanted to tell her how everything had gone, and what Art and Joe had said. I wanted her support; I wanted her objectivity. And I wanted to *laugh*. It seemed like ages since I'd seen her.

I walked quickly through town to the café and burst through the door. Maggie spun round from the sandwiches she was making and screeched "You *cow*!"

"*What*?"

"Keeping me in suspense all this time! A whole sodding week, Coll!"

"Oh, Maggie, Christ, I—"

"I've been *desperate* to know what happened – like being eaten up by *maggots*. For a whole sodding *week*. I tried to get your phone number off Bill and d'you know what he said? He couldn't give out the personal details of his staff. Look you tight git, I said, I know more about Coll's personal details than anyone on this earth. In that case, he said, you can look up her phone number. So then I had to admit I didn't know your stupid surname. So then he gave me that smirk he does and walked away!"

"Oh, Maggie," I giggled, "I'm *sorry*. I've been so wrapped up in—"

"Coll, just tell me! Did he turn up? Did you whack him one? Did he grovel? Beg you to go back with him?"

"Well – he said – he might call –"

"He did? Patronizing shit. You want him to?"

Just then two noisy well-dressed couples arrived, wanting food and coffee, and Maggie mimed slitting her throat and hissed, "Later!" But before they'd gone, more people turned up, and then there was a steady flow of customers throughout the evening. Maggie and I raced about like cartoon characters, serving and clearing, and she'd fire questions at me – "You still fancy him?" – that I'd only be able to answer five minutes later. "Yes – worst luck – *YES!*"

Then, an hour before closing time, the café emptied out apart from a large, self-absorbed group by the window, and Maggie came and stood beside me. "OK. Tell me *all*."

"Oh, God. Well, it's not good. I mean – I was hoping I'd feel different when I saw him, you know, cold, but I felt –"

"Hot."

I laughed. "Yes. Very. And messed up. And angry. And upset."

"Does he seem different?"

"A bit. He's gone all surfy. Says things like 'score some surf'."

"Oh dear."

"Yeah. All he could talk about was New Zealand. Nothing about us. And then I met his friend Joe, and apparently he's been sleeping with millions of girls out there –"

"Oh, *lovely*."

"Oh, *God*, I don't know. He's just – he's just –"

"Coll. Why don't you start at the beginning, and tell me what happened."

"OK," I said, but before I could draw breath the café door crashed opened and Art and Joe walked in.

Chapter fourteen

"Hi Coll," Joe slurred, "We need coffee *badly*!"

"Hi," Art said.

I felt so totally betrayed by Joe I could barely look at him. What was he *doing*, telling Art where I worked, *bringing* him here, without warning? I couldn't show this, though – I had to keep my cool. You're allowed to feel betrayed when your friend sleeps with your husband or sells you into slavery or something. Not when he asks for a cup of coffee.

"Hi," I said, as they staggered over to the counter. "You're drunk."

"Yes, we are," Joe agreed happily. "We're celebrating Art leaving home. He moved into my place today."

"Oh," I said. "That's a bit sudden, isn't it?"

Art looked at me, expressionless. "The old man blew up. Again. So I left. What about those coffees, Coll?"

"Oh, sure. Right." I turned away, blundered towards the coffee machine, pressed the buttons, filled the jug, poured the coffee. I could hear the cups rattling on their saucers as my trembling hands conveyed them to the boys. I had this brief fantasy of

89

tipping the scalding liquid forward and into their laps.

Joe and Art had climbed on to high stools at the counter and slumped across it. Joe thanked me for the coffee, then leaned forward and slurped all the froth off without lifting the cup to his lips. "We shouldn't . . . have had . . . that last . . . beer," he groaned.

"Joe said he'd seen you," Art said, flatly. "Yesterday."

I met that like a challenge. "Yeah. We went for a drink." I turned my back and started to wipe down the coffee machine. "It was good to see him again."

"We've been on a pub crawl," announced Joe.

"I'd never've guessed," I retorted. "So – does your dad know you've moved out?"

"Dunno. Don't care," Art said, then he fell silent, and I turned back to face him. He was sending a silent, concentrated stream of energy towards me. Like a blowtorch. I don't know how he did it. Well, I do. It was in the hunch of his shoulders, and his stare, as he looked at me from underneath his dark eyebrows. They were such strong lines on his brow, matching the lines and shape of his jaw, his cheekbones.

He watched me, and my brain kept telling me: *It's over, over. Think of him with all those women. Think of him with Maria.* But my eyes kept sliding back to his face, back to his eyes.

90

Then Maggie appeared at my side and saved me. "Gonna introduce me?" she said.

"Sure," I croaked. "This is Art, and this is Joe. This is Maggie – she works here."

Maggie was brilliant. She start just *chatting*, acting so nonchalant and laid back she was practically asleep. I let all her words buffer me; I crouched behind them. I hadn't got my shell on, not like the first time I'd seen him. I hadn't had time to prepare it. So everything about him was going straight in, deep in. And he was drunk. Not as drunk as Joe seemed, but the alcohol had changed him. He kept staring, sending out this energy. It was like he had no shell on, either.

We managed to spend fifteen minutes talking about anything, nothing, and then Maggie said she had to close up.

Joe wrung another coffee out of her, then, at last, the two of them headed for the door. Joe was full of drunken half arrangements and promises to phone. Art said: "See you, Coll," but I didn't look at him, I couldn't. When Maggie had finally shut the door on them and locked up, she came over to me and put her arm round me. It was so good, that contact. "What was going on there?" she said.

"I don't know. I don't know what he's playing at."

"He looked like he was trying to hypnotize you."

I started to cry then; I couldn't help it. I was so

tense and wound up. "He doesn't have to," I sobbed.

Maggie tightened her arm round my shoulders, and steered me towards a nearby table. "Come on, sit down," she said. "Tell me what's going on."

We talked and talked, long after we should have shut up the café and left, all about how my meeting with Art had gone, and what Joe had told me, and what it all meant. Twice Maggie got up to fetch more coffee. She turned all the lights off but one tiny one in the kitchen so that people walking by wouldn't see in and think the café was still open. We didn't come to any conclusions, of course. Not about anything. But I felt so grateful to Maggie for giving me her time once more.

I tried to apologize for going on so much, but she waved it aside. "It doesn't matter, Coll," she said. "What matters is where you're at now, and what decisions you're going to make."

I smiled at her. "God knows. I feel about a million miles away from making any decisions about anything. Come on – we should go. You've been great, Maggie. You must be shattered."

We stood up to go, and she murmured, "You should keep away from him, Coll."

"I know," I said.

Chapter fifteen

I had the most powerful dream that night. I was by
the sea, watching it break on the shore. Crash, crash,
crash. And then I knew someone was behind me,
watching. And I knew it was Art, before I even
looked round. As soon as I turned to look at him, he
started to walk away. I shouted after him, but he just
kept walking. So I followed, running and shouting,
but he didn't turn round. I followed him into a cave.
The sea was coming in, the tide was rising. I knew he
was in the cave, I could feel him there, but I couldn't
see him anywhere. The water was getting higher and
higher and there were all these strands of seaweed
caught on the rocks that started to float out as the
water reached them. Then I heard a shout, and I
looked up and there he was, on a ledge above me.
And he leaned over and reached out a hand, and I
took it and he started to haul me up. I was scraping
my legs and arms on the stone and I was really scared
he'd let go but he kept hauling and I kept scrambling
up. Then I got to the ledge, and I felt his breath on
my face, and I wanted him so badly; I wrapped myself
round him, really tight. There we were on this tiny,
wet, seaweedy ledge, and the water was rising

beneath us. And we started kissing and he was so warm against the cold, wet stone, and all I wanted to do was make love before we drowned. I started pulling off his clothes, and pulling him down on to me, because all that mattered was to have him inside me before we drowned.

I felt bloody awful when I woke up. Disorientated, frustrated, tearful, and angry at myself for dreaming that stuff. I didn't exactly need to call Freud in to tell me what it meant, where it had come from.

I felt almost panicked, being in my room. I got straight out of bed and hauled on some baggy old sports gear. Then I went downstairs, grabbed an apple, got my bike out of the garage, and left before Mum could arrive and press-gang me into helping her cook the Sunday morning family fry-up.

I know I sound like someone out of a *Girl's Own* manual, but when I'm really messed up, I have to do something physical. Biking, or running, or swimming, or walking fast – it all helps. I stop thinking; I take comfort in my body's rhythm, in getting more and more tired. And then sometimes, solutions come to me.

For the first twenty minutes I just switched off and pounded the pedals, then I began to look around me, watching the day as the sun warmed it up. The fields were looking green and spring-like, throwing off the dusty old coat of winter; the air was full of birds calling to each other. No solution came to me this time, though. I couldn't get beyond the feelings of the dream.

When I got back, Mum directed me to a plate of wrinkly looking bacon and eggs in the oven, and told me Val had phoned. "She asked me if you were free tonight. I told her you were."

"Well, thanks, Mum," I said, sarcastically.

"You can always tell her otherwise! You should see her, though. Do you good."

"*Thanks,* Mum," I said again, and she sailed serenely out of the kitchen.

I scraped the bacon and eggs into the bin; just the sight of them made me feel ill. Then I showered and got dressed and wandered around in my room, picking things up and putting them down again, unable to sit still, unable to start work. So I went downstairs to phone Val.

I felt quite nervous as I dialled her number. I'd kept her completely in the dark about the fact that Art had come home, and if she found out she'd be so upset with me life wouldn't be worth living. *I can't go on like this with her*, I thought, as I listened to the ringing tones. *Something's got to give somewhere.*

"Coll, hi! Thanks for phoning back. There's a party tonight."

"Sunday night?" I said, dubiously.

"Yeah. Don't come over all school-the-next-day on

me, I've already had that from Mum. It's not a big deal. Rachel's house is free – her parents are out till late. It won't be a party exactly – she doesn't want too much clearing up."

"Who's going?"

"Oh, you know – the usual crowd. She's getting food in, she wants us to bring some booze."

"Oh, OK, then. Great." No point arguing. And anyway, it would fill the time in, and with luck there wouldn't be anyone new there that Val could try and force me to get off with.

I was kind of living on the boundaries of the dream I'd had all day, restless and mournful; threads of it were still clinging to me when I got to Rachel's house that evening. I think that's why it was such a shock to walk into the kitchen and find Val and Greg acting like they'd like to kill each other. Rachel was practically cowering in the corner.

"Not that plate," Val snarled. "It's not big enough."

"OK, you know what you need – you get it."

"Jesus, Greg, it's not *that* difficult. I just need a plate for this stuff. . ."

"Val, if this is the sort of mood you're going to be in all evening, I'm going home now."

"Mood? What mood? All I said was I needed a plate for—"

"It's the *way* you say it. Like I'm brain dead or something. Like the smallest thing is beyond me."

"Ha! You said it, mate."

"You've been in a shit mood ever since I picked you up tonight."

"I have *not*! Jesus, just 'cos I don't fall about all over you, you think I'm in a bad mood. God – *I'll* get it. Just leave me alone."

I stood in the doorway waiting to say hello. And I couldn't find any sympathy in myself, for either of them. I was thinking: *Who the hell d'you think you are, spilling this out over us all. You should control it.*

Then I marched into the kitchen and said, "Hi, Rachel. Here's the wine. Put it in the fridge, yeah?"

"Hi, Coll," said Greg. "Did you come on your bike?"

"I walked," I said. "Hi, Val. Can I help with that?"

"It's done."

"Anything else need doing?"

"Well – I was going to cut up that French bread—"

"Here, I'll do it." I started slashing into the bread, crumbs flying, then I piled it into a bowl Rachel silently put down next to me. Anger was sparking off me. I couldn't really explain why it was there. It felt good, though, in a way. I felt alive.

The door knocker cracked three times, and Rachel sped off to open it. Soon the kitchen was filling up Caro, Chloe, Richard, Dave, Mike – all the old crowd, plus half a dozen other people I knew by sight. Someone started handing round cans of lager, then Rachel ushered everyone into her tatty old back room, and turned up the music. I grabbed the wine I'd brought from the fridge and found myself a fat glass. Then I picked up the bread I'd been slicing and a big dish of tacos, and followed on.

For the first fifteen minutes or so, I concentrated on drinking. It was what I felt most like doing. I was sitting on the floor near Mike and Richard, half joining in their dumb conversation that went from football to music to football again. I felt OK, as though I had a right to be there.

Then Rachel slid over across the floor to sit next to me, like I knew she would. She'd been watching me since I'd arrived, as though she had something big to impart or big to find out, or maybe both.

"I saw Joe the other day," she said, quietly. "In town."

"Yeah? You speak to him?"

"Yes. I was in HMV, and he wandered in –"

"How was he?"

"Fine – he said he was fine. Uni going well and everything."

"So – any regrets?" I smiled at her. She'd gone out with Joe briefly, last year. I'd sort of fixed them up together.

"No. Well, he's nice. But – you know. It didn't work then, so. . ." She breathed in hard. "Look – Coll. He had Art with him. He said he was . . . he said he was *staying* with him."

I took another glug of wine. "Yeah. I know."

"You know?"

"I've seen him. Art called me. I saw him again."

Rachel looked at me in stunned silence. Then I heard a kind of eruption of horror from the sofa behind me and I turned to face Val.

"You *saw* him again?" she choked out.

"Hi, Big Ears. Yes. I did."

Val's face was a scream. I almost laughed. "I don't *understand* you, Coll. After all he did to you –"

"I saw him because I wanted to."

"You wanted to. After the way he treated you."

"Look – I was curious. How he was and stuff."

"*Jesus H. Christ*! Who *cares* how that complete bastard is?"

"Val, he isn't a complete bastard. He's just more or less screwed up, like the rest of us. No – he's more screwed up. More screwed up than me, anyway."

"Oh yeah?" she snarled. "You've been so messed up these last months you can barely move!"

I shrugged. "Yeah, well. Maybe that's why I needed to see him."

"Honestly, Coll," she snapped. "I just *do not* understand you. I thought you'd have more pride than to— What d'you want to go raking all that up again for, it's like – *God*. It's so *unhealthy*."

Maybe it was the revulsion streaming from her, but something in me snapped. "What makes you think *you're* so healthy, Val?" I said. "You should look at yourself sometimes – you and Greg."

She glared at me, full of anger. Then she got to her feet and stalked towards the door. I scrambled to my feet. Greg stood up too but I kind of pushed him back on to the sofa; I clambered over his legs, going after her before he could. "Let me *talk* to her," I said, then I went out and shut the door behind me.

She'd gone into the kitchen and was standing there by the sink, back towards me. I couldn't tell if she was crying or not. "If you've come in to apologize, you can get lost," she said.

"I haven't," I said. "I meant it."

That made her turn round. I took a deep breath. "Val, we just can't talk to each other any more, can we." She was silent. "I know you've tried to help these last months," I said. "No – you *have* helped me. But – there isn't only one way of doing things. There really isn't. I saw Art because I—"

"I don't want to discuss it. I'm sorry, it disgusts me."

"Oh. Great."

"Well it *does*. He snaps his fingers and you *jump*—"

"That's not true—"

"I give up on you, Coll."

"Fine. Give up on me. I just wonder *why* it makes you so angry. Why it all has to be the way you do it. I know I've been a mess but—"

"A mess? You've been a complete wipe out."

"So you're *always, always* telling me!" I was almost shouting now. "I mean – I know I must've been a total drag, but did you *really* think making me feel even worse about myself was going to help me?"

She glared at me. "I've done trying to help you. You won't help yourself. And I think it's pretty shitty of you to throw all the times I've phoned you up and got you to come out with us back in my face—"

"Oh, *Val*! Look – I told you – I was grateful – you did it because you cared, and I was grateful you wanted to help me – it's just – I felt so *steamrollered.* Like my opinion didn't count. I mean – you were great at first, a great listener, but then you decided I'd lost it completely or something—"

"You have. Seeing him again proves it. You've lost it."

"No – I *haven't!*"

"It's so *weak*, Coll!"

"Oh, *Jesus. You* don't have the slightest idea what I went through, deciding to see him again. You don't understand why we split up."

"Oh don't I?"

"No! Not really! You just want to think – he's a bastard, Coll's a victim. Well, it's not that simple. Nothing is. I don't go along with that black-and-white, he's-wrong-I'm-right level, not any more – I'm not going to live my life on that stupid level. You can, if you want."

"Look Coll – sometimes you have to make decisions and stick to them."

"All right. But maybe not knowing is an OK state to be in for a while, maybe it's *not* weak, maybe it's *strong*—"

"I told you – I don't want to talk about it." She sounded really cold. I watched her as she stalked towards the door, then turned back to me. "And I can do without your snide comments about my relationship with Greg, as well. We're fine."

"No you're not," I spat. "What about tonight – here?"

"That was a row. So?"

"So you're *always* rowing! You just chip away, scrape away – and you're *always* like that. It's awful, Val, insane. You don't notice any more, because you do it so often. It's *vile*."

"Oh, *right*. So I'm vile now. Well, poor Greg, having to put up with it."

"Val, this is about you." I could hear my voice cracking. "It's vile what's happening to you. You've become this – you're all bitter, and closed in, and it's like you're punishing Greg. Every day, every time you see him – it's like you're *locked* in this thing together. . ."

She took a step towards me, and her eyes looked

like they might ignite at any minute. "Yeah, well, we are, aren't we. Locked in it together. *If* you remember."

"Yeah, I do." I felt close to tears. "I was there."

Then Val spun away from me again and there was a horrible silence; then this awful, animal wailing came out of her, and her shoulders started shaking like an earthquake. I jumped forward and grabbed her, and held on to her as tight as I could, and the relief I felt was amazing. Something had cracked; something had broken through. I felt like we were being honest at last, at long last. "It's OK, Val, it's OK," I kept saying. "It's going to be OK."

"Leave me alone," she howled. "Leave me *alone*." She pulled away from me, and practically ran out of the door.

I didn't follow her. I heard the front door slam.

Chapter sixteen

Greg appeared in the kitchen almost immediately. "Coll – what happened? What the hell did you say to her?"

I knew that in the end I was going to get the blame for everything, but I didn't care. Right then I was too churned up to care, about anything. "Oh – lots of stuff," I said. "She ran out."

"I should go after her," said Greg. He sounded as though it was the last thing he wanted to do.

"I upset her," I said. "I'm sorry." I wasn't though, not really. I was just sorry she'd run out, before we got a chance to really talk.

Greg stood there, twisting his hands together. "Look – I ought to go," he repeated.

"I'd leave her," I said. "She'll go home. It's not far and the . . . the walk'll do her good."

"But suppose she's outside, s'pose she's just – out there."

"Go and have a look. If you can't see her, come back."

I waited in the kitchen with my heart pounding. No one else came in to see what had been happening. Maybe they were oblivious, or maybe they were all standing listening in the living room, gazing at each other, mouths open in shock.

After less than five minutes, Greg reappeared. "I can't see her," he said. "I went to the end of the road, and looked along the high street, then I came back and looked around the house. . ."

"Why don't you give it half an hour, then phone her house," I suggested. He groaned. "Or I will. Make sure she's safe."

"Yeah. Oh, God she—"

"Greg. It's not ten o'clock yet, and it's Sunday night. She'll be fine."

"Yeah. God. What on earth did you say to her?"

"Um. We got a bit heated. She told me I was weak and mad and stuff, 'cos I've seen Art again. So I told her . . . I said. . ."

"You told her what you thought of what's going on between us."

"Yeah. And don't tell me it's none of my business. She's changed so much. She's all – bitter and critical, over everything, not just me. She's just not *happy*."

He glared at me. "What about me – d'you think I'm happy?"

I sighed, shakily. "No. Neither of you are."

There was a silence. "So what did you say?" Greg asked. "What made her freak like that?"

"It was – it was . . . Greg, I can't remember what we said exactly. I'm not even sure we said anything, clearly. But what made her run out, it was about the . . . about the. . ."

"Abortion."

"Yes. She said something about being locked up with you, and then she *really* broke down, I've never heard her cry like that. I put my arms round her but she just shoved me off and –"

Greg walked heavily over to the kitchen table, and picked up a bottle of wine that was standing there. Then he peeled off the top, and opened the wine, then went to the cupboard, and pulled out a teacup. "You want some?" he said, over his shoulder.

"Yes please," I whispered.

He put two teacups on the table and filled them to the brim. Then he handed one to me, pulled out a chair, and sat down with his head in his hands.

I pulled out a chair opposite him and sat down too, and waited.

He downed a whole teacupful of wine, poured another one, then he looked at me. "She won't talk to me about it. It's like it's there, all the time, but it's become this taboo. And whenever there's anything on the telly or anything that comes anywhere *near* it – she'll freeze up. Or walk out. I got to dread that sodding advert – insurance or something – where the dad finds a pregnancy kit and blows up at his daughters and it turns out his old lady's the one who—"

"Yeah," I said. "I've seen it. She looks about seventy, and she's going to have a kid."

"Yeah. I knew Val was thinking – she's having the baby, they don't even think about abortion. It was like – it was like it was criticizing her."

"So you think she regrets it? Doing it?"

"I don't know! I just told you – she won't speak about it. Well, she did at first. She exploded once, really badly, and then we got all close, and she cried a lot, but she said she'd done the right thing, and it was like we were going to pull through it together. But then things just got . . . colder. She wouldn't talk, she said she'd got over it. But she hadn't."

I had the sudden thought that, over the last six months, in our own ways, both Val and I had been trying to get over something by denying to everyone that it was there. It made me feel weird. "It doesn't work," I croaked. "You can't make something go away by just . . . ignoring it. You think you're being strong . . . but all you're doing is pushing it down. It takes so much energy, too – pushing it down."

"Yeah, well, Val has no energy for anything any more – only fighting with me. I wish she'd – if only she'd talk to someone about it. I mean I think it's part of the problem, that nobody really knows. It's like – it's almost like she's pretending to be someone she's not."

"Someone who didn't have an abortion."

"Yeah – oh, I dunno. I only know she'd die before she'd let her mum know what happened. And she's made me swear not to say anything – Caro and people, they don't know. Only you. There was this woman at the clinic who said she could call her, any time – some kind of a therapist, it's part of the deal they do – and I said a while back that she should give her a ring. *Jesus*, the shit hit the fan then. She kept accusing me of thinking she was having a breakdown, cracking up, when all I'd said was—"

"She won't talk to me either," I murmured. "But then I've been. . ."

"Very wrapped up. In other things. Yeah. You know what – I think she thinks both of us, you and me, have let her down in a big way. You because you were so miserable you couldn't help her, and me because . . . me because. . ."

"You got her pregnant."

"I don't know. Maybe. Except it's like something that's happened *since* then. Oh *God,* it's horrible. I feel like shit most of the time. When I try to talk about it, what's going wrong with us, she gets very angry, upset . . . so I shut up, and it's . . . it's bringing us both down, Coll. I mean – it's making us really small. It's –"

"Demeaning."

"Yeah. We're acting out this horrible, fake stuff together. And I can't see a way out."

I took in a deep breath. "I think – I think you should both finish it. I think you should have a break from each other."

He laughed, hopelessly. "That's easy to say. There's *no* way I'd do that to her. There's no way I'd – suggest it even. Or let her know I was thinking it. There's no way I—"

"OK, *OK*. There's no way."

"She wants out. Sometimes. Only just for a night or so. She wants to go to clubs on her own. I hate it. It's like – it's like she wants to hurt me. I mean – it would be OK if I didn't think that was the reason she wanted to go, but. . ."

I looked down at the table, then I took a long pull of wine from my teacup. Greg and Val made me think of two people drowning, clinging together in the sea, going down faster because of the way they held on to each other. I couldn't think of any way out for them.

"We've made love three times since it happened," he suddenly announced. "It was a disaster each time. Now I've given up on it. I can't even cuddle her properly in case she thinks I'm trying it on."

"Oh, Greg. That's—"

"Don't tell me it'll get better. It's like – written in stone, now. Like our whole relationship."

I looked at my watch. "I'd better phone her, hadn't I. Make sure she got back safe."

"Yeah. Would you?"

Chapter seventeen

"Mrs Sparks? Hi – it's – it's Colette."

"Coll? Hello, my love." There were still traces of soft Irish in Val's mum's voice, even though she'd come to England twenty years ago. "Don't worry, Val's here. She got back five minutes ago."

"Oh – is she? Oh God. That's good. She just . . . she. . ."

"Did she have a row with Greg or something?"

"Er – yes. Yes, she did, and. . ."

"Oh dear. I don't know. It's all they seem to do, nowadays. I've told her – cool it for a bit. Have a break, at least until the exams. She won't listen, though. Says I don't understand."

"Oh. . ."

"All I understand is, none of it's making her happy. Look – she's gone to bed. I won't disturb her, unless you really –"

"Oh no – no, don't. I just wanted to check she was all right. . ."

"You're a darling," Mrs Sparks said. "Why don't you call her tomorrow. Talk some sense into her for me, eh, Colette?"

When I got back to the kitchen, I saw that the wine

bottle was nearly empty. Greg was slumped forward on to the table, gazing into his teacup like some crazed fortune teller.

"It's OK," I said. "She's back home. I talked to her mum. She said Val'd gone to bed."

"Oh, right – good. Thanks, Coll."

There was a long silence, and I was just rehearsing how I was going to tell him I was taking his car keys off him, when he suddenly said, "What was it like?"

"What?"

"You and Art. Sex. What was it like?"

"Oh Greg, for God's sake –"

"I watched you once, at a party."

"*Whaa-at?*"

"Oh Jesus. Not actually – you know, only leading up to it, idiot. Kissing. It was one of those parties we had at the beginning of the summer – you remember?"

I stared at him, wondering what on earth he was going to come out with next. But I did remember the parties. Art and I spending all our time together, after his exams. That sense of wildness, school's-out relief.

"He was leaning down towards you, and you had your neck bent so far back your face was like – it was at right angles. And he kept going down on your neck like a . . . like a fucking vampire. And you loved it. You loved it, Coll."

111

"Greg, you are really, seriously drunk and I'm going to. . ."

"You were wound up so tight together – you kept moving closer together. I don't now how you got any closer, but you did. Everyone in that room was watching you, and you had no idea. Either of you. You didn't care. Why should you. You kept pulling his head down on to you – you had your fingers right into his hair, he had his hands – Jesus. Everywhere. Then you left. You must've gone somewhere and shagged each other senseless."

I continued to stare at him, concentrating on not crying. My eyes felt like two hardboiled eggs, swimming in brine.

"Sorry. Sorry, Coll. D'you miss him?"

"Yes," I whispered.

"So it was good?"

"Yes."

"It never got really good. Not for me and Val. We never had time . . . we never. . ." He let his head fall forward on to his arms, and I thought he was crying. I reached over and stroked his arm, awkwardly. "It was OK, because neither of us knew what the hell we were doing at first. Absolute beginners. And we were both so crazy about the idea that we had each other, that we were lovers. . . But we never had time to practise . . . we never . . . we never got fired up. Not like you."

I crept out of the kitchen, and went back into the party room. About a dozen pairs of eyes turned to me, then looked away, studiously incurious. I went over to Dave, who had to be the biggest, strongest lad in our group.

"Val's gone," I said. "And Greg's legless. Can you. . ."

"Got his car keys?"

"I don't think we need to. I'm not sure he can even stand up."

"No problem, Coll. I'll walk him back."

"You might have to carry him."

"Yeah, well. He can collect the car tomorrow night."

"Yeah," I said, gratefully. "That's what I thought. Look, thanks. I'm off too."

Then I slipped out, not even saying goodbye to Rachel, and sped home, running for most of the way, running so I wouldn't have to think.

Mum met me in the hall, in her massive green candlewick dressing gown. "You're back early!" she beamed. "Good time? Oh yes – before I forget – JOE phoned again. We had quite a nice chat. Who is he, Colette? I think he's rather jolly!"

Chapter eighteen

It was not easy, getting to school the next day. At registration, I was not a bit surprised to find Val was absent. I suspected Greg would be off from his school too, nursing the mother of all hangovers. I decided I'd go and see Val straight after school. All day, I thought about her and what I should say to her. I remembered what Maggie had said, about Val needing help, and now I was there lined up to give it. I knew I had to somehow save what had broken open between us last night.

And into my head every now and then would surface the fact that Joe had phoned, too. I was eaten up with curiosity about what he wanted to say to me. And whether Art had been standing by his side when he'd called – whether it was really *him* calling me. I didn't get a lot of work done.

When I got to Val's, Mrs Sparks seemed very pleased to see me, which made me feel terrible. If she knew that it was me who'd sent Val spinning off last night, I thought, would she still be as welcoming? I didn't know. Maybe she would.

"She's just sat up there all day," said Mrs Sparks, pushing her hair back anxiously behind her ears.

"Won't speak to me. I hope you can get some sense out of her."

"Did . . . did Greg come over?" I asked.

"No. But he phoned. Poor lad. She wouldn't speak to him. Here – I've just made some tea – would you like a cup? You can take Val up one too."

There was a silence as Mrs Sparks poured out two mugs of tea and got some biscuits out of a cupboard. Val's three little brothers and two dogs appeared the instant they heard the biscuit wrapper crackle. Mrs Sparks cut the packet in two, gave half to the kids, and put the other half on a tray with the tea. Then she handed it to me and said "Good luck" in a weary, ominous sort of way.

I thought Val was asleep when I first walked in. The curtains were drawn and I could make out a long, hunched shape under the duvet on the bed. The room had this stale, sad atmosphere in it.

"Val?" I whispered. "You awake?"

There was a sort of moaning sound, then Val rolled over. I couldn't see if she was looking at me. "Can I pull the curtains?" I said. "It's really dark in here."

No reply. I put the tray down on her desk, walked over to the window and pulled the curtains halfway back. A band of pale, late sunlight crossed her bed, just missing her face. Then I put one of the mugs of tea down on her bedside table and said, "Val? How are you?"

No reply. Minutes passed. "Drink it while it's hot," I said. Then: "Are you going to speak to me, or not?" Still no reply. I picked up the half packet of coconut biscuits and ate one, noisily. "You may as well speak to me. I'm not going to go away."

I could hear mumblings from under the duvet, and I knew I was getting there. "What you saying, Val? You want a biscuit? They're good."

Her face appeared. "No, I *don't* want a poxy biscuit. Why are you here?"

"To see you."

"Look – can you just go away, Coll. I feel like shit. I don't want to see *anyone.* Please. Just go."

"OK. In a minute."

"No. Now."

"Nope. It's my turn to bully you."

That made her sit up. "If you've just come here to make stupid, snide little jokes you can—"

"Oh, *come on,* Val! It's *me!* Stop farting around and talk to me. What are you doing – staying in bed until it all scabs over again and you can go back to how you were before?"

She stared at me, hostile. "I don't know what you're talking about."

"Yes you do. What's going on? What happened last night?"

"What do you – you *know* what happened last night. I flipped. I freaked. You upset me – I ran out."

"Yeah – but what was going on inside, Val? What made you do it?"

"Oh, for *God's* sake –"

"I think it was good you flipped and freaked. I prefer you flipping and freaking to all that control you were into before."

"Well I *don't*. I hate it. And you're just saying that 'cos you've got *no* control."

"You're right. I'm putty. Weak as this tea. Art phones, and I jump, just like you said."

"Coll – please. I don't want to talk. Just go."

"Greg said some things last night," I murmured.

I could sense her wrestling with herself.

"You know . . . we got talking."

"What . . . what did he say?" she whispered.

"About how he doesn't think you've come to terms with it," I blurted out. "The abortion."

She went rigid. "You . . . you had no right to. . ."

"Oh, *bullshit*. He loves you . . . I love you. He got you pregnant. I was there right after you'd had the operation. If *we* can't talk about it together, who can? He reckons your problem is you don't talk enough, and I agree."

"Oh, yeah," she said bitterly. "*Talking's* really going to solve it all."

"Well, what is, Val?"

There was a long, long pause. She was twisting the duvet cover this way and that between her fingers. I thought it would rip under them at any moment.

"What you said last night," she suddenly began, hoarsely, "you're right. It's shit. The way we are together, it's horrible. I'm horrible. It's just – negative, destructive." She looked at me, anguished. "We don't have fun any more. We can't. I ruin everything. And I feel like I'm in this trap, this . . . just going round and round. . ."

"So. . .?"

"Don't tell me to end it. I can't."

"Why can't you?" I said gently. "What are you scared of?"

"Feeling even worse than I do now," she said, beginning to cry. "If that's possible. Letting go of the one guy who has to. . ."

"*Has* to. . .?"

She looked at me defiantly, and it was as though she was seeing something for the first time. "Yes. Has to. He has to put up with how I am. It's his . . . it's his *fault.*"

There was a pause, then I said, "No wonder you've been feeling bad about yourself, Val, if that's the way you see it." She didn't answer. "Haven't you thought," I went on, "if you *weren't* with him, you'd be OK? There wouldn't *be* anything to put up with?"

"What?" she snapped. "I don't know what you mean."

"It's just . . . you seem to think all the snapping and snarling you do is just down to you. All your fault. But suppose it's there 'cos of the mess you've got yourself into with Greg?"

"Jesus, Coll, it's too late to talk about that. It's, happened, hasn't it."

"I don't mean the . . . I don't mean the abortion. I mean the way you are together, what's going on between you *now*. You said yourself you feel trapped, and it's awful – don't you think you'd feel better if you got out of it?"

She looked down. "I don't know. I can't take the risk."

"Oh, Val."

"Sometimes it's good with Greg. Sometimes I get so low, and he just holds me and. . ." she trailed off.

"If you'd had the baby," I said suddenly, "how old would it be now?" Val looked at me like I'd hit her. "Two months – three?"

"Why are you saying this, Coll?" She was staring at me, her eyes brilliant, pain-filled.

"I'm trying to say – you still feel it, don't you. But you won't let yourself admit that you do. You're like some – pressure cooker, honestly, holding it in all the time. One day soon, you're going to explode."

She turned away from me and stared out of the window. "Maybe it'll never go away, not completely," I went on. "Maybe you'll have to accept that, and face it, and . . . and adjust to it. But that has to be better than just *denying* it, like you're doing now. It won't get better with Greg, it can't, not while you're holding all that down."

Val continued silent. I took in a deep breath and realized how tired I felt; tired from all the tension of the last forty-eight hours, tired from trying to work all this out. "I'll go and get some more tea," I said. "Shall I?"

I crossed the room and had my hand on the door knob when she said, "I hate him for what he did. I can't help it. I still hate him."

I turned, came and sat down again.

"He pushed me into it. He said he'd be careful. We were baby-sitting his little sister, and we made love as soon as she'd gone to bed. Greg was really pissed off because he came too soon. Then we had a bit to drink and we got going again, only we'd . . . we'd run out . . . I told him he should go out and get some more Durex . . . he said there wasn't time. He said his mum and dad were getting home about eleven. So we . . . we did it. He withdrew. Look – he didn't rape me. He didn't even pressure me, not that much. Only inside my head – I knew I should say no. I knew I was doing it because he'd got so passionate and he was desperate to make it better this time, and . . . being *wanted* like that was. . ." She stopped, and a huge tear trickled down her face.

I reached out and got hold of her hand. "Well, that was pressure, Val."

"Yeah. It's like – you're the woman, you be the policeman, you be the one that says no. It's not fair. Well, maybe it's fair with some sleazy pick-up, but it's not fair with someone who says he loves you, someone who. . . Anyway. We had two huge rows about it. One before I had the abortion. . ."

"Yeah, I remember. That's why you wanted me to come to the clinic with you instead of him."

She squeezed my hand then slightly, with her thumb, and I felt a rush of hope, as though at long last the barrier between us was crumbling. "Yes. And then we had another one later – a really awful one. I never told you about that."

There was another long silence, and she pulled her hand gently away from mine. "So are you going to tell me about it now?" I asked.

"It was – oh, into the summer. Exams over, school out – we should have been feeling good. And he wanted to make love – the first time since the – you know. And I just *turned* on him. It was dreadful. I was like – I went mad. I scared myself. I certainly scared the shit out of him. I said I hated him for what he'd done, and I'd never trust him again, and all that stuff . . . and then after hours, it felt like hours, we just held each other and cried and talked. And somehow, I don't know how, it all got explained away as letting go of what had happened, you know, clearing the air. And I felt so grateful to him, for not finishing with me, for still being in the same *room* as me, after I'd freaked like that – that I told him I didn't mean it, and I said I knew it'd been both of us, we'd both been stupid, and he said we'd taken the risk because we were so crazy about each other and how it would only . . . it would only bring us closer . . . and so. . ."

I gazed at the closed curtains, seeing them together, frightened, desperate to heal things. "You kind of agreed an explanation between you," I said. "Like a pact."

"Yeah. It was like that. Only at the time I thought I really felt it too. I mean – I *felt so* close to him again. I really thought I'd forgiven him and moved on and stuff. But then . . . oh, maybe a fortnight later, something happened . . . I can't even remember what. He pissed me off. And I felt this rage in me, I can't tell you – as though I wanted to kill him – it scared me, I wanted to scream all this stuff at him again, just like before, all the same stuff."

"And did you?"

"No. I was so . . . so *appalled* by what I was feeling, so frightened, I just clamped down on it. I thought – if I let it out, then we really will be finished."

"But if it was so awful, what would've been so bad in finishing it?"

"Oh, Coll, don't keep asking me that! I don't know! I was scared – I thought I was going mad or something – I didn't want to be on my own! And – I don't know – I thought if I broke off with him – then it would've been like admitting that the whole thing had been a disaster. I dunno – if I could save our relationship, then maybe the whole thing wouldn't be such a waste, such a mistake . . . I s'pose I wanted to believe the stuff about the abortion only bringing us closer."

"Even though you *knew* – underneath, you knew it hadn't."

She shuddered. "Yeah. Even though. It happened again, lots of times. Every time he pissed me off it would . . . *surface*. I mean – I've always had a temper. You know."

I smiled at her. "Red hair."

"But I'd sit on it. I never really let it out."

"Pressure cooker. See – I was right. Oh, Christ, Val. How can you keep seeing him with all that between you? You never told him? When you were like – *calm* – you never tried to talk about it, tell him you couldn't help blaming him still?"

"No. It sounded so nasty, crazy. And . . . you know, I didn't want to break that . . . that *agreement*, that everything was all right again, that we'd got over it. Even though it was fake."

I shut my eyes for a minute, trying to get my

thoughts clear. "OK, so you lied to him. It was like –
an ongoing lie. Lots of people do that with people
they care about. I reckon it does most harm to the
person doing the lying. It like – it *clogs* you. You
pretend you like his parents, when you think they're
pigs . . . it brings down this barrier about all kinds of
things, I reckon. It doesn't let things flow between
you. . ."

"Yeah, OK, OK," sniffed Val. "I know."

". . .and with you, you're making yourself act like
you've forgiven Greg – but you *haven't* – it's like a lie,
and it's a big weight on you, all of you. And all the
anger built up . . . you had to let it out or you'd
explode. It had to come out somewhere else . . . in
little ways . . . that's where all the rows came from."

"Yeah. It got to be a habit, the way we were. Like
we'd forgotten it could be any better. I don't know
why he didn't dump me. I don't, really."

"'Cos he has an incredible sense of loyalty to you,
that's why. And because you used to be so good
together. I think he feels as trapped as you do, Val.
Just as lost."

She let out a sigh then, long and low, as though
she was letting go of something. I stood up. "I bet
you could do with another cuppa, couldn't you,
now?"

She nodded, head bent, and I went downstairs to
the kitchen. Her mum was in there, spooning mashed

potato over a massive shepherd's pie, and she looked up, full of hope and enquiry, as I walked in.

"All right if I make another pot of tea?" I asked.

"Of course, love," she said. "You go ahead. So – she spoke to you, then?"

"Yeah. She's – it *is* Greg. She's really screwed up about whether to finish with him or not."

Mrs Sparks nodded. "I thought that was it. He's been her first real boyfriend. They were so thick at one time it . . . well, it worried me." She shook her head, carried on spooning. "Young love. It half kills you, doesn't it."

I tried to agree, but it came out like a snort of grief. "Thanks, Colette," she went on. "For letting her get it off her chest, I mean."

I climbed up the stairs with the tea-tray, went back in Val's bedroom, and poured the tea. "It can't be easy, with your mum and dad being Catholics and everything," I ventured, handing Val her mug.

"Oh, Coll. They're not exactly hard-liners. How d'you think they only had four kids?"

"No, but I bet they don't exactly approve of abortion."

She shrugged. "No. Well – it's not something we talk about, really."

No, but it's there, I thought, *under the surface. Deep, at your roots.* She hung her head, and I thought she'd started crying again.

"You could've talked to me more," I said gently. "Why didn't you?"

"Oh, Coll! You were in no state to think about anyone but yourself! And anyway, I didn't – I didn't want to admit to it. Not even to myself."

I gazed down at the pattern on her duvet, frowning, trying to make the right connections inside my mind. "These last couple of months, we've both been doing the same thing, haven't we?" I murmured. "We've both been trying to carry on and pretend nothing was wrong and we'd recovered. Only . . . you made a better job of it than me. Which means a worse job, I think. I mean . . . a more damaging job."

The light was going from the room, but Val didn't turn her lamp on. She sighed, and it came out in a long, shaky breath. "I hated you," she said simply. "Some of the time I just . . . *hated* you."

"Why?"

"I hated you for sinking down, the way you did. It was like you were being – I don't know, self-indulgent. Wallowing in it all. And then you started to pretend you were OK, and you never looked at me straight and . . . I hated you more, then. I s'pose underneath I felt really guilty. For not being open with you – not letting you be open. The whole thing – the way you were – it scared me. I thought I could go that way too. I had to tell myself you were just being weak."

"I wasn't weak," I said. "I just really loved him. I still do."

"I know," she said, and she got hold of my hand, and we sat there together in the darkening room.

Chapter nineteen

Before I left Val, I made her promise to at least think about phoning up the woman counsellor at the clinic and maybe going to see her. I said I'd make the call for her, find out if it was OK to make an appointment after such a long space of time. "Although I'm sure it is," I assured her. "It's not like there's a sell-by date on it or something."

I managed to stop myself suggesting she broke things off with Greg for a while, too. I thought she had enough to deal with, and I didn't think things could go on like before with him anyway, now that this had happened.

She curled up under the duvet once more as I made my way to the door, looking as though she wanted to sleep for ever. I told her I'd see her at school tomorrow, but I somehow doubted I would.

I got back home at about seven o'clock, and Mum met me at the door, bursting with a nauseating mixture of curiosity and what almost seemed like flirtatiousness.

What a pity you weren't here five minutes ago!" she announced. "That young man phoned again! Joe!"

"Oh – right."

"He *does* sound nice."

"Mum – OK."

"Are you going to phone him back before supper – or after? Only it's nearly ready."

In answer, I stomped up to her bedroom, shut myself in, and dialled Joe's number. I had it scribbled on the back of my school diary.

He answered, almost immediately.

"Joe? It's Coll. Mum said you'd phoned."

"Coll! Hi!" He sounded really pleased to hear from me. "Yes, I did. Twice."

"Yeah. Mum said you had a nice chat with her, the first time. She thinks you're *jolly*."

"Oh God, that's bad."

"Yup. Pretty serious. She hates most blokes but if she *likes* you – well. It's a bit of a stigma, Joe."

"Oh God. I always do great with mothers. It's the girls themselves I don't get anywhere with. Er – look, Coll. I really phoned to apologize. For – you know – for—"

"Bursting into the café with Art. Too right you should apologize. I nearly passed out."

"Well, you carried it off OK. Honest."

"Did I? Thanks. But what on earth made you. . .?"

"Look, I was really drunk. Maybe you noticed."

"Kind of," I said dryly.

"We just – we got completely pissed together. And

129

Art started talking about how he'd seen you, and how good you were to talk to. And when I reminded him what he'd said about steering clear of trouble and stuff, he just went on about you being a friend and coming to terms with the past and that's when . . . that's when I found myself saying you were working in this café, nearby."

"Oh. Great. Well done."

"Yeah. Then I don't really remember what happened next. Suddenly we were out of the pub and in the centre of town and going into Perk Up. Crap name, by the way. I mean, it's too deliberate and it's kind of twee, it's—"

"*Jo–e!*"

"Sorry. Yeah, there we were. And after, Art said how good it had been, you know, dropping in on you, no big deal, just like mates. . ."

I was silent. The last thing Art and I had been that Saturday night was mates. Unless in the primal sense. I remembered his eyes, lasering across the counter towards me. I remembered how I couldn't look at him and breathe at the same time.

"Anyway," Joe went on, "he seems to want to be all mature now. He's phoned his dad, and come to some sort of a truce, and he's got himself some building site work—"

"*Building* site?"

"Yup. Like the work he was doing off and on in

130

New Zealand. Pretty brainless, macho stuff – just up his street. Keeps his muscles toned and his tan going. Pays well. He even offered my mother rent, that's how grown up he's being, but she wouldn't take it. Just a bit for food. I tried to get the money off him later, told him she'd changed her mind, but unfortunately he twigged and—"

I laughed. "Joe, shut up."

"Yeah, OK. But it's worked out well. The old lady's even told him he's welcome to stay on for a bit, after I've gone back to uni."

"Wow. What's he doing, cleaning the toilets?"

"Stacking the dishwasher. And being charming. I'm taking lessons, I tell you. Anyway, Coll?"

"Yes?"

"The reason I'm phoning, apart from to say sorry, is to ask you to a party this Friday."

"Yeah? Whose?"

"An old mate of mine from school. His parents have gone away for the weekend so –"

"So he's taking the chance to trash the house once they've gone."

"Well, not quite. They actually said it was OK for him to have a party. As long as he fed the cats when they were away."

"Blimey. Nice parents. Well, great, Joe. Who's – who else'll be there?"

I meant "Will Art be there?", and Joe must have

known it, but he burbled on for a bit about some of his mate's college friends and some of the old crowd from school, and then he said, "I don't know about Art, Coll. I mean I have to ask him, don't I. If he came – would you not want to?"

And then I heard this voice, coming out of my mouth, that was me and not me. "Oh, it wouldn't make any difference. He's right – it's in the past. I've got to get used to just seeing him around, haven't I. Especially if he's going to be staying on."

"Whoa. So mature, Coll."

"I'm trying to be."

"That's not how you were talking the other night."

"No, but – you know, after you came to the café and everything, it seemed, I dunno, less intense." Jesus, what a liar.

"Well, OK. Good for you. Look – ask your friend from the café too, if you want. She was a laugh – good to talk to.

"Maggie? You fancy her or something?"

"No. That's why I could talk to her."

So I said I'd ask her, and Joe gave me the address for the party, and I put the phone down, and scurried downstairs totally freaked. *Oh God*, I thought, *what happened there? What* – possessed *me, literally?* I didn't mean to start lying to Joe. To pretend it didn't make any difference whether Art would be at the party or not when it was all I cared about, all I could think about.

I sat down at the kitchen table and fended off Mum's enquiries about the phone call and chewed my food like an automaton.

Chapter twenty

Val finally turned up to school on Wednesday, and she looked better. Rested, determined. At lunch time we escaped to one of our old spots behind the gym, a bench between two skinny trees and the bike racks with their groups of smokers, and she told me she'd written Greg a letter.

"Blimey, Val. Heavy."

"I know. I feel such a coward. But it was the only way I could be sure I'd be straight with him. You know, without backing down into play-acting and everything's-all-right again."

"So – what d'you say?"

"Oh – just I thought we should have a break for a while. Because I'm so messed up about everything. I didn't go into details, but I think –"

"He'll know."

"Yes. And I said I was sorry for being such a bitch the last few months, and I told him – I said I was making an appointment to see the woman at the clinic. Just to talk."

"Oh, that's good. That'll please him."

"I'm going to phone up tonight, when Mum's out."

"That's great, Val."

There was a silence, then I said, "So you didn't tell him you still blamed him, or anything."

"No. Because – because that's part of me being messed up. I know it is. I told him not to contact me. Not for a while, anyway."

We watched the sparrows hopping about on the concrete flagstones, looking for sandwich crumbs. I imagined Greg opening the letter, and the mixture of grief and relief he'd feel when he read it. "D'you think you can keep to it?" I asked, gently. "Not seeing him, I mean?"

"I've got to. I think I can. It feels so good just to have got this far, made this decision. I feel kind of empty but – good." She turned to me. "Coll, you really helped me the other day. Coming round. Not letting me kick you out. And at Rachel's – you know, when you laid into me about being warped and everything?"

I laughed. "I didn't say you were *warped* –"

"Whatever. Unhealthy, you said that. . . Well, I was. And I was thinking about the other stuff you said – about how we'd both been doing the same thing? You pretending you were all over Art, and me pretending everything with Greg was fine."

I shifted in my seat uneasily. "Yeah?"

"Well, it's no wonder we couldn't speak to each other properly. We'd always been so straight with one another, and then suddenly we were just lying, about everything."

"Yeah."

"I'm sorry I was such a cow to you, Coll. Remember when you ran out of that party?"

"Mmmm. You and Greg came after me in the car and I thought you were going to whack me one –"

"I nearly did. You *scared* me. I think part of it was . . . you know. I wanted to run out too. Oh, I'm *glad* that's all over, Coll. I'm glad we've got over that. I missed you."

Cue for a hug. I felt so pleased, so relieved, as we wrapped our arms round each other and then fell apart laughing.

But I knew I was still lying – I don't know how I met her eyes. They looked wet. "We're starting over, both of us," she said. "No backtracking. And we've got to be honest with each other from now on, right, Coll?"

"Right," I said.

"I need to start getting out without him, seeing a new crowd," she went on. "Breaking the pattern."

"Yeah, you must. You must, Val." This would have been the perfect opportunity for me to tell her about the party on Friday. Friday was the day we broke up for Easter, and it could have been a nice celebration. But I didn't, because if I did, I'd have to tell her that Art might be there, and then she'd tell me I couldn't possibly go. And she'd be right.

I just mumbled something about a new club

opening on the other side of town, and said nothing. Some friend, eh? Some new start.

I'd lied to Joe, I'd lied to Val; I wasn't going to lie to Maggie. That's what I told myself as I headed over to the café that evening. I threw myself through the door, waved to her, went behind the counter and helped myself to a coffee.

"News update, Maggs," I said. "Want to hear it?"

She laughed. "What *now*?"

"Art's moved into town indefinitely. He's got a job, he's staying at Joe's house, he's charmed the pants off Joe's mum –" I stopped. "Well, not literally."

"You sure?"

"Sure. I hope."

"Only from what you told me, he's got chronic satyriasis."

"Chronic *what*?"

"Satyriasis. Typical, you don't know what it means. Everyone knows what a nymphomaniac is, but no one knows about satyriasis because it's meant to be bloody *normal*."

"You mean it's when you're a *bloke* and you want to do it all the time? Well, that *is* normal."

"Yeah, right. It's a medical condition, Coll. After satyrs – those goat men from the myths, with pointy beards and enormous –"

"Dicks."

"– noses and chins. Yes. They say Kennedy had it."

"They do?"

"Yup. He was unstoppable."

We'd started to get the giggles. "Look, shut up, Maggie. You want to hear the rest of my news or not? There's a party Friday night, and Joe's asked me to ask you."

"And Art's going to be there, and you want to go."

"Right. And I know I shouldn't, but I want to, I *have* to, and I'm going. So save your breath."

"OK, OK, I won't say a thing. You have to go through this lunacy, I can see that, Coll."

"Right. And will you –?"

"Yes. I'll come. I'll watch over you. I'll scrape you off the floor and take you home in a plastic bag."

"Thanks. *Pal.* Seriously, Maggs, I want you to come."

"I'll come," she said.

Maggie and I arranged to meet at a pub a short walk from the party. I'd changed my outfit about twenty times before I was satisfied I was giving the right effect. Gorgeous, but relaxed. Special, but everyday. Oh, God help me. I didn't dare even look at what was going on inside me. I felt like I'd started falling and I was waiting for the impact.

My jaw nearly hit the floor when Maggie walked into the pub. She looked so different from usual.

She'd put some sort of gel in her short, blonde hair and slicked it back, and she had weird earrings and make-up on, and purple nail varnish. And black trousers, and boots, and a bright top under a black leather jacket. It was sexy and strong but kind of funny, playful, all at the same time.

"Wow, Maggie," I breathed. "You look –"

"Fantastic. Go on. Tell me."

"*Different*. And fantastic. Yeah, you do." The whole get-up really suited her. The colour on her eyelids brought out the strange green colour of her eyes.

"Well, thanks. You look great too. You'll slay him." She leaned towards me, joke-threatening. "If that's what you want to do."

"I told you, I don't know what I want to do."

"No chance you'll give the party a miss, and come clubbing with me instead? I mean – I spent hours getting ready. I kind of feel it's going to be wasted at some house party."

"No chance. And you *won't* be wasted, Maggie. If it's that bad, maybe we can go on to a club later."

I knew I was bulldozing her. She knew it too. "OK," she sighed. "Get another round in."

I was totally hyper and not a little drunk by the time we got to the party. And I knew from the minute we walked in it had the potential to be great. It had just the right music, just the right lack of lights, just

the right sprawled out, unplanned, interesting feel
to it.

It was good walking in with Maggie, too. I felt
outrageous just by association. You could feel people
turning round, checking us out.

I knew no one there. I'd told the guy who opened
the door that I was a friend of Joe's and he'd just said
"Who?" and opened the door wider to let us in.

"I don't think they're here yet," I hissed to Maggie.

"No. Come on." She headed into the kitchen and
fought her way through to where the booze was. I
was amazed by how confident she was. When Val and
I used to turn up at parties together, we'd *act*
confident all right, but inside we were quailing. The
more intimidated we felt, the snottier we'd behave.

But Maggie seemed totally relaxed right through.
She poured out a couple of glasses of wine for us both,
and grimaced at the two blokes on the opposite side of
the table. One of them was opening a lager bottle with
his teeth. "How can you *do* that?" she said.

He shrugged, then grinned at her a bit stupidly.

"You won't grin like that when half your teeth are
broken," she said amiably, and turned away.

"C'mon," I said, "let's go in the other room. Where
the music's coming from."

On our way through the hall, the front door
opened, and I spun towards it. "Down, Coll," Maggie
murmured. "It's not him. Now *relax*."

We wandered into the main room, peering into the gloom. It was pretty crowded; everyone was in tight little knots, talking loudly above the noise. And then, with a great stomach lurch, I spotted Art. He was standing by the bay window, with Joe and two girls.

"There," said Maggie, nudging my arm. "You want to go over and say hello?"

"*No!*" I hissed hysterically.

"Why not?"

"Because – because we can't just barge in! He could be chatting her up!"

I felt sick just at the sight of it. One of the girls was standing about a millimetre away from Art. She had her head on one side, looking up at him. I swear that there are deep elements in us that have never caught up with the whole civilization process. All I wanted to do was race across the room with some kind of heavy weapon, and fell her.

"I shouldn't've come," I wailed quietly. "I'm going to have to watch him getting off with someone, aren't I. Oh God. I want to go."

"Coll, calm *down*. Jesus."

"I hate this. I hate feeling jealous. I feel like I'm being disembowelled."

Maggie turned to me, and actually laughed. "You are one of the most extreme people I've ever met, you know that?"

"Sorry."

"No, I like it. It's OK. Now look. What we're going to do, we're going to go outside for a minute and take in some deep breaths? Yes? And then you can decide whether you want to stay, or go home, or, best idea, go on to a club and forget all about it, OK?"

I gazed at her gratefully. "Yes. Thanks, Maggie. Oh God, I'm sorry. I thought I could carry this off."

She started to tow me towards the door. And just before we reached it, there was a kind of eruption to the left of me, and Joe was bursting through the crowd saying "'Scuse me – 'scuse me – Coll! Hi, Maggie! You made it!"

A split-second glance showed me that Art was behind him, and the girls weren't. I needed all the self-control at my disposal not to let my knees fold under me and my body crumple on the floor.

I can't remember what sort of small chat went on between Maggie and Joe. All I know is, Art was standing there, a bit apart, and I was standing there rigid, not looking at him, and then Maggie had her hand on my arm and was practically dragging me out of the room.

"We're getting another drink," she hissed. "And then we're going outside like I *said*."

Chapter twenty-one

Outside, I let myself sag against the cold wall.

"Jesus, Coll, you have got to get a *grip*!" said Maggie.

"I know, I know. Why did you drag me off like that? What were you saying?"

"I dragged you off because you looked like you'd just been *headbutted*. And we weren't saying anything. Just hi, hello, see you later."

"He'll go back to that girl," I moaned.

"Coll, I am going to *slap* you in a minute!"

I looked at her face, half laughing, half angry, and started giggling.

"That's better," she went on. "Now look. I don't know what's happening. I don't know if you want to get back with him, or just get used to seeing him around –"

"Me neither," I groaned.

"– but I do know you've got to stop acting like an idiot. We either go back in that room and you *face* it – or we should go. Maybe we should go."

"No. Maggie – no. I can't just run away. I'm fine now, honestly."

I was anything but fine, but I wanted to get back

in the same room as him. I needed to.

The music had got louder when we got back in, and people had started dancing. Maggie gave a kind of approving whoop, and got hold of my hand, and dragged me to the side of the room where there was a bit of space. Then she started dancing. She was wild. Some people, when they throw themselves around like that, look embarrassing and awful. But she was really at one with the music, taken up by it.

I started laughing and dancing with her, copying what she was doing. "That's it!" she crowed as she gyrated next to me. "You're here to boogie – not keep mooning after that git."

"Can you see him?" I whined.

"*Coll!*"

"*Sorry!*"

We danced on, three more songs. Then one came on that I knew I could jive to. Jiving, I have to tell you, is one of my skills. My Uncle Max taught me when I was a kid, and over the years I've done a lot of practising and I like to think I've improved my technique.

I seized Maggie's hand and started putting her through the paces. She latched on immediately – I could tell it wasn't the first time she'd jived. Some people have the knack, others don't. We did a bit of musical shoulder barging, and soon we'd cleared a space big enough to really let rip in. Three blokes were leaning up against the wall, watching us. Joe kept swinging past, making funny comments – he seemed to know everyone in the room. *I hope Art's watching, too*, I thought. *I hope he can see me having fun without him.* I'd tried to teach him to jive a couple of times, and both times it had ended in disaster, and then him grabbing me and all thought of dancing disappearing.

Two more pounding records, and Maggie said, "Let's go and get another drink. I'm *hot*! This party isn't as dud as I thought it was going to be."

I'm calm, I said to myself, *I'm coping.* We headed for the door; I gave myself the task of not scanning the room for Art, and almost succeeded. Then I walked into the kitchen and nearly collided with him.

"Hi, Coll," he said.

I couldn't speak.

"The beer's all gone," said Joe triumphantly. "Most of it down my neck. Oh God, I'm pissed."

"*Again?*" said Maggie, mock-appalled. "What is it – something about being a student that means you have to be rat-arsed half the time?"

She walked over to the tap and filled two glasses. I watched her every move as though I was going to have to sit an exam on it later, because I didn't dare look anywhere else. When she handed me the glass, I drained it.

"No wonder you're so hot," Joe said helpfully.

"You were throwing yourself about out there."

Art was standing there silently, engulfing me. "I'm – I've gotta find the bathroom," I muttered. I put my glass down on the draining board; Art stood back to let me pass. I felt my back prickle as I turned and left the kitchen.

I headed upstairs. The bathroom door was open, and the light was on. I scrambled inside, shot the bolt to and subsided against the door with a long shudder of relief. Then I had a quick pee, washed my hands, and leaned towards the mirror.

My eyes looked weird. Not just because I'd drunk too much. They looked other-worldly weird. Wide with tension. I'd left my bag downstairs, but I rifled shamelessly in the little wooden cupboard hung over the sink and found a comb, which I ran under the tap and then through my hair, and some mascara and neutral-looking lipgloss. I looked OK when I'd finished. I smoothed down my clothes and took in a deep breath.

He's outside, I said to myself. *He's followed you upstairs; that's what you wanted him to do.*

I unlocked the door and stepped out on the landing. Art was standing by the banisters. "Hi," he said. "Did you find the bathroom?"

"Yeah," I answered. Then I waved inanely towards the bathroom door, and said, "There."

"Thanks," he said, but didn't move towards it. I

took a step towards him. "You're looking good, Coll," he went on. "It's good to see you again."

"Yeah," I stammered. "You too." Desire, that learnt reaction, was spreading inside me.

"I hope you weren't too pissed off, when I moved into Joe's."

"Why should I be?"

"Oh – I didn't know if you'd want to see me around. You know."

"It's a free country," I said, stupidly.

He laughed. "Yeah. So – you all right?"

"Yeah. Fine. What about you?"

"Better. Really, better. I've got away from the old man, I'm earning –"

"Yeah, I heard. What are you, a hod carrier?"

"Something like that. Next week I sort out college."

"Wow. Dynamic."

He smiled; I stared at his mouth as the corners lifted, and I wanted him so badly I felt as though it had driven out everything else, everything. Then he said, "I like your friend."

"Maggie? She's great."

"Those dykey types can look dead horny."

"*Dykey?* She's not dykey."

"Well, she looks it."

"Oh, *God.* Just 'cos she's got those boots, and likes leather, and—"

"You. She likes you." He was grinning at me, knowing, sneering. "You dance really well together."

"Thanks," I said, coldly.

"Maybe it's her hair that makes her look dykey."

"Oh, for *Christ's* sake," I exploded, and he started to laugh, and couldn't help it, I joined in. "It's great, her hair. I love it. I keep thinking I'm going to get all mine cut off, I—"

"Don't, Coll."

"What?"

"Don't get your hair cut."

There was a long, long pause, during which I knew I should get away, get back to Maggie and Joe and safety, but I didn't. "How are Greg and Val?" he asked.

"Oh – bad. They split up." I started to blunder through a quick precis of what had happened to them. *We're doing it again*, I thought. *What we used to do back in the beginning. Making stupid small talk, while the real communication went on silently. Physically.*

"I missed talking to you," he said, suddenly. "When I was away."

"Yeah," I said.

"It's great we can – you know. Still talk like this."

"Yeah," I said. "It's great."

Chapter twenty-two

Up on that landing was when the entirely fake platonic friendship between Art and myself was silently agreed on. Definition of platonic = free from physical desire. There we were, standing close, exchanging enough energy to fuel a rocket, and somehow we were able to agree that we just liked *talking* to each other. That we'd moved beyond what was, and become friends.

It was so totally fake it was a masterpiece.

I knew why I'd unspokenly agreed to it. I was buying time. At the same time that my good sense told me to cut all ties, I had this hunger for him, this fierce nostalgia, that demanded to be fed. I wasn't sure about his motives. Maybe he *did* just want to talk to me. But I didn't think so.

Fairly soon, I peeled myself away and went back downstairs, acting out the role of the person who's had an unimportant friendly chat on the landing. Art wandered off to the bathroom, then he reappeared in the kitchen, and soon all four of us were talking half-heartedly again. Joe was the centre, as usual. Without his jokes, his easiness, we would have been a strange group. Maggie was fizzing with quiet hostility towards

Art; he faced her down with a sullen sort of stare and occasionally he baited her, slyly. I didn't say much, because talking just wasn't the point for me, then.

The party had taken a down turn, and people were drifting off home or going on to a club. It was about 1 a.m. Maggie said we should go, and I agreed. I felt exhausted. As we were leaving, Joe said maybe they'd look in on us at the café again, tomorrow night.

"OK, you want to club it?" Maggie said, as we walked arm-in-arm along the road.

"No."

"What then?"

"Just walk."

It was a cold, clear night. We had a good half hour trek in front of us, but that felt fine. "You were talking to him, weren't you, up on the landing?" Maggie said. "He went slinking out after you."

"Yeah, a bit," I said. "Just chat. It made it more – I dunno, normal. I still feel – you know, I haven't exactly forgotten what we had together. But I've got over the shock of seeing him again and now it's OK just having him around, it helps somehow." I shut up then, because I realized I was using that voice again, the one I'd lied to Joe and Val with, the possessed voice, the ventriloquist's dummy's voice.

We walked on a bit, and I added, "It's not as though he's going to be around for long."

"Isn't it?" said Maggie. "That's all right, then."

* * *

He was around the next night, though. He and Joe pitched up at the café an hour before closing time, and took two seats at the counter, just like before. And, just like before, they'd had too much to drink.

Maggie was cool and slightly disapproving. "This is getting to be quite regular, isn't it?" she said, rather acidly. And then: "Honestly, you bloody students. It's taxpayers like me who pay your grants."

Joe beamed at her vacantly, trying to work out if she was being funny or mean, and Art said, "So you're not a student, Maggie?"

"Nope. I was – art – but I dropped out after a year."

"So you work here full time?"

"At the moment, yes." Maggie sounded hostile, as though she didn't like being cross-questioned. And I felt this great pang of guilt that that was the first I'd heard of her being a dropout art student. I knew so little about Maggie or her background. It was my fault. I never seemed to find the time to ask her. Still, now was not the time.

"What made you drop out?" Art asked smoothly.

"Oh – stuff."

"Yeah? What stuff?"

"Just stuff."

"So the café's better?"

"For now, yes."

Art started asking her how long she'd worked here, what she thought she'd move on to, and Maggie stood against the sink, barely answering him, secret and closed up as an oyster. Art circled her with his words, with his looks, prodding, prying, trying to get in.

And I didn't like it. I didn't like it at all. It wasn't that I thought he was trying it on with her or anything, I just didn't like it.

Maggie didn't like him, that was clear. She was as coolly hostile as she could be without being downright offensive. And Art's voice took on a sneering, teasing tone, to both of us. It was just getting really uncomfortable when Joe said, "Oh, blimey, nearly forgot!" and started fumbling in his jacket pocket. "Tickets," he said. "Wednesday night. There's a gig over at Hampton – not far. Schroedinger – d'you know them?"

He flipped four square red-and-black tickets on to the counter, and I gazed at the name on them and felt like I'd crashed back in time. Schroedinger was the band that Art had taken me to see, on our first ever date together.

"I'm still in touch with the bass player," Art said. "He got us the tickets."

"I know Schroedinger," said Maggie. "They got in the charts not so long ago, didn't they." She picked up one of the tickets and examined it. "Blimey, fifteen quid. You had to pay for these?"

"Art never pays for anything, do you, mate?" said Joe. "He just phoned up and asked, using all his nauseating and overpowering charm."

"I wanted to see them again, that's all," Art said. "I knew they were playing this area."

"So, you two going to come with us?" Joe went on. "I'll drive. And –" he looked at Maggie – "I shall remain entirely sober all night."

"You better," said Maggie.

"Apart from the intoxication caused by the music, of course."

Maggie groaned, and asked what time it started, and then we were all talking as though we'd agreed to go. Maggie was sure she could get Wednesday evening off; we arranged where to meet and what time. Then Maggie said, "It's nearly closing time, Coll, throw everyone out. Especially these two. I'll start on the kitchen."

I skirted the few occupied tables politely, murmuring about shutting up shop. At the counter, Art and Joe remained immobile. They were the last to walk towards the door, and I followed them to bolt it. Joe walked out first, shouting goodbye, then Art turned back to me and said quietly, "Those tickets – I'm not trying to take you on some cheesy nostalgia trip."

"I didn't think you were."

"I just knew I could get free tickets."

"Yeah – well. That's great."

He grinned, suddenly. "You remember them?"

"Yes. They were good."

"Yeah. I remember you enjoying it." Then he said, "Night, Coll," and left. And I realized I was leaning back against the door with my hands trapped behind me in a posture that could have headed a list called: *"Body language: offering yourself to the male."*

"Shit," I muttered, stamping back to the kitchen.

"I'm not sure about this foursome thing," Maggie said, elbow-deep in suds. "I mean – only yesterday you were nearly passing out over him at that party – and now you say you're just friends?"

"Oh, it'll be OK. Really, Maggs. And it's a one-off."

"You are *so-oo* better off without that guy. He's all looks and dick."

I laughed. "Come on, he's not the point. The free tickets are the point. They're a great band."

"I s'pose."

Chapter twenty-three

I didn't look at what I was doing. I didn't want to. I worked hard Sunday, then I met Val in the Dog and Duck that evening. She was still in a new-beginnings mood, all hopeful and looking forward. Then she showed me a card she'd had from Greg. It was big and rich-coloured, with a picture of a pre-Raphaelite red-haired beauty on the front.

"Go on, open it," she said. "Read it. I don't mind. He wouldn't either."

I shrugged, and opened the card. "Thank you for your letter," it said, in Greg's scrawl, but neater than usual. "You're being incredibly strong. I'm sad but I know you're right. If you need to see me, I'm here. I won't stop loving you, Val. Greg."

"Aw," I said. "That's lovely."

"Isn't it. It's kind of – freeing, but like he's still there, too. Oh God, I just feel so much better, Coll. About everything. I really do. I've made an appointment, too, at the clinic."

"You have? That's great."

"Yeah, two weeks' time. They didn't turn any sort of hair about me leaving such a long gap, either. It made me feel – I dunno. Normal."

She smiled at me across our glasses of lager, and I smiled back. And when she invited me to agree with her about how good it was to make a fresh start and free yourself from the past, I agreed with her.

I half horrified myself. My single-mindedness, my ruthlessness. No woman hiding refugees in her cellar put up a better lying front, a more innocent face, than I did.

That night, I had another dream. I was walking through this strange, crumbly old castle, and I went into a big, empty hall with windows high in the walls, light falling down from the windows on to the floor. Then I saw there was something in the corner. It looked like a cage; it was half covered by an old tapestry or something. I knew something was in it, something alive, before I could see it.

I got closer, and saw it was a wolf. A great grey wolf just sitting there, looking at me, full of sadness because it was in a cage. I went up to it and rubbed its head, pressed against the bars, then I put my hands through the bars and stroked it, although I felt very scared. Its fur was amazing; thick, crackling. I started to feel so excited, so turned on, and I had my hands right through the bars, stroking it, stroking it, and it started to lick my bare arms with its rough tongue, and I knew how much it wanted to get out, and I wanted to let it out, but when I looked at it, I felt scared. That was all I remembered. It was such a strong feeling. It was stronger than any feeling I'd had for days.

I woke up sweating. You didn't need a degree in dream psychology to know that I'd been dreaming in code, and the wolf was Art, was all that I felt for Art. And I wanted to let it out.

And then there we were, in Joe's car, acting the part of four mates who were just happily and unimportantly together. Joe and Art sat in the front; Maggs and I in the back, Joe doing most of the talking. Once we'd got to the hall where the band were playing we bought drinks and stood about for a bit, Joe still chatting, Art and Maggie niggling at each other, me silent. Then the lights went down, and we found a place to stand as close to the stage as we could.

Schroedinger shuffled out to a big burst of yelling and clapping. They waved sheepishly, keen to be musicians, not stars, and went through the testing and tuning routine. Then they started to play, filling the hall with sound, and I could relax into being who I really was.

Joe was standing between me and Art, but he kept moving forward as he jerked about to the music. A real beaty one came on, and this seemed to put Maggie in a good mood; she started to move too, laughing, next to Joe.

Art turned his head to look at me. He raised his eyebrows, mouthed, "Glad you came?" I nodded, and looked towards the stage. The space between us crackled. I could sense him drawing closer to me, lessening the space.

This undercurrent, this exchange, went on throughout the concert. No touching – the energy was stronger than any touching. At the interval, I was like someone on some kind hallucinogenic drug, inhabiting my own reality, only just managing to hold it together for the outside world. Art was taciturn. We hardly looked at each other. The four of us went through the charade of getting drinks and discussing the band; I ran to the loo ahead of Maggie so she couldn't corner me and question me, make me leave the world I was in.

When we went back to stand in front of the stage for the second half, Maggie stood between Art and me, but the link was still there. Schroedinger got into some of their older stuff; a really slow bluesy one started up. It was one that had got into the charts, and everyone clapped at the opening bars. Art turned to me behind Maggie's back and mouthed "Remember this?"

I remembered it. I remembered swaying to it, winding my arms round his neck, intoxicated by the feeling that I was touching him at last.

And then I knew it was going to happen again. I

knew I could make it happen. It was like being starved for months, and then shown a way to get food.

The band finished, the hall erupted in applause, the band came back for an encore, the lights went up over the second burst of applause. And Maggie took my arm like a possessive sister. "Let's go," she said. "Come on, Joe. I told my folks I wouldn't be later than twelve."

"It's only ten past eleven," Art said. "I'd like to go and see if I can say hi to Alex. The bass player. I haven't seen him for months."

"Can we all go?" asked Joe.

"Well – maybe four's a bit of a crowd. Look – I won't be long. I just want to say thanks for the tickets." And he loped off.

We wandered over to Joe's car, and he and Maggie got into a half-hearted discussion about the cost of running it. Then Joe said, "Oh, for heaven's sake, where is he? What's he up to?" and Maggie said, tartly, "Holding us all up, that's what. Let's go without him."

"I'll go and get him," I heard myself say. I sounded so casual, it was masterly. "I know the way backstage."

As I walked away from the car I was waiting for Maggie to shout out, "What the hell are you playing at, Coll? Come back." But maybe they had no suspicions. Maybe they thought I really was just going to bang on the dressing room door and tell Art to hurry up.

Well, maybe I was.

There were quite a few people still milling about in the dingily lit corridors: roadies lugging equipment, groups of girls talking excitedly. I was barged from side to side as I made my way along. I turned a corner, and heard noises of celebration coming from an open door at the end, so I headed towards it.

It was the dressing room for the band, chock full of people, waving arms and cans of beer, laughing raucously. I hovered nervously in the doorway, waiting for some huge bouncer to come and evict me. Then I spotted Art just inside the room, talking to one of the band. Alex the bass player, presumably. Art glanced up. "Hey – Coll!" he called, raising his arm, reaching his hand out towards me.

I walked towards the hand, and it came down warmly on my shoulder. I walked closer still, and it moved round my neck, pulled me up against him.

"Hey, Coll," he said, happily. "You found me."

"Yeah," I stammered. "Joe's getting –"

Art turned to the bass player. "Alex, this is Coll."

"You were great," I said fervently to Alex. "You were so good tonight." Alex grinned pleased, and Art's arm tightened round my shoulders. "They're getting pissed off waiting, Art. We'll end up having to walk home."

Shit, I made that sound like an invitation. "I'd better get packed up," Alex was saying. "I'm knackered. Art – next time we play here – I'll send tickets."

"Yeah," Art said. "Please." Then he looked down at me. "We'd better go, then."

I was waiting for him to slide his arm away from me, but he didn't. He steered me towards the door, along the corridor. There were still so many people careering along it, carrying stuff, shouting, you could just about explain the arm as protective, gentlemanly. Then there was a shout behind us; "Watch your backs!" A mean-looking roadie was trundling a massive pair of speakers towards us on some kind of trolley. Art did a kind of jack-knife round me, and pulled me in towards the wall. We were standing face to face against the wall, his arm still round me. The roadie and his trolley thundered past.

I couldn't speak. I moved closer. I was going to make it happen.

He didn't speak either, but he always did everything best in silence.

He pulled me in closer still and wrapped his arm round my back. I tunnelled my arms underneath his jacket, tight round his chest. Then I looked straight up at him. He gave a funny little sigh, and muttered,

"Missed you." Then he bent his head down, and I reached up, straining for his mouth.

We kissed, and I was in an ecstasy of remembering. His taste, the way he moved, it was so right, nothing had changed. Response on response on response. Still the same, just hungrier. Needier.

Then there was a shout like an axe, breaking us apart. Maggie's voice, spitting, "Joe's driving off in two seconds – if you want a lift home." I looked up guiltily just in time to see her stalking off, back down the corridor.

We started to walk after her. Separate, space between us. We didn't speak. Why didn't we speak? Why didn't he *say* something? *He's regretting it*, I thought. *He's regretting it already*. We got to the car in time to see Maggie wrenching the back door open and sliding inside, and I followed her. Art got in the front and muttered an apology to Joe, who said "It's OK, mate, it's OK" and started up the car.

Maggie sat glowering in the back. I glanced at her rigid profile, and the initial guilt I'd felt wavered, and anger started to take its place. We drove on in silence. Joe made an attempt at a couple of light comments, but they kind of withered on the air, so he snapped on the radio, loud.

"*Jesus,* Maggie," I hissed, under cover of the noise. "It was just a kiss!"

"Sure," she snarled. "Just for old times' sake,

right? After all you're just *friends*, aren't you?"

"Look – it just – *happened*. The music, and everything."

"And you're glad it happened. You want to go back."

"I don't know," I muttered, my eyes on the back of Art's head. I could still taste his mouth. "*I don't know*."

She turned her face to me, vivid with anger. I almost quailed at the sight of it. "Jesus, Maggie, what *is* it? I don't understand why you – I don't see why *you—*"

"Drop you off here, Maggie?" Joe interrupted cheerfully from the front.

"Yes," she called out. "Please." Then she turned to me again and muttered, "OK, Coll, I'll explain. You meet me after work tomorrow, and I'll explain."

Chapter twenty-four

Joe pulled up and Maggie shot from the car, calling out "Thank you" back over her shoulder before disappearing into the night. Minutes later, Joe pulled up outside my house. He turned off the engine and swivelled round in his seat to beam at me. "OK, Coll?" he said.

Art turned round too, but I couldn't meet his eyes. I looked up from under my hair and took in his mouth, which was half smiling, then I lunged sideways and grabbed the door handle. "Thanks, Joe." I sounded half strangled. "Thanks for the ticket, Art." Then I half fell on to the pavement and scuttled up the path to my front door.

Safe in my attic room, I paced. From the bed to the door to the skylight and back again. Then I realized if I kept it up I'd have Mum lumbering up the stairs insisting on knowing what was wrong, so I sat down knock-kneed on the edge of the bed and contracted every muscle I knew how to, hoping I might relax a bit when I let them go.

I didn't though. I felt tired, but still as tense as ever. I was eaten up with curiosity about Maggie and her over-the-top reaction, and I was desperate about

Art. It took me hours to get to sleep, hours. Then I woke in the morning too early, and the night before came flooding back, and I got out of bed, all panicked and displaced. I crept over to my desk and sat down at it. It hit me that the Easter holidays were here and very, very, terrifyingly soon I'd have A levels to deal with and if I didn't watch out I'd flunk the whole lot of them just because my emotional life was in such a mess.

I stared at the pile of files stacked up in front of me. I hadn't touched them since we'd broken up, five days ago. I shifted them a little to the left, patted them. We'd had all the lectures at school about starting revision early, using the holidays well. "It's here, it's all here," I muttered, as though I was soothing a madwoman, "you've done the groundwork. You just need a clear head for the next couple of months."

Hah. Some hope of that.

I got through the next day, I got through the early part of the evening, and then I walked down to the café about half an hour before closing time. Maggie waved, smiling, when I walked in but she was too busy to come and speak to me. I collected some coffee, took a seat at a small out-of-the-way table and waited. When it was time to close I helped her clear up as quickly as I could.

She filled two mugs to the brim with creamy coffee, turned out all the lights but the one from the kitchen, and we sat down at one of the tables. Then she grinned at me like a fox, and said, "Maybe I overreacted last night."

"Maybe," I said, a bit sulkily. "Anyway. What have you got to explain to me?" Vague fears were circulating in my mind.

"It's just – I can't stand your ex, Coll."

"Well that's not exactly news, Maggie. I mean – I'd kind of grasped that."

"OK. More than that. I *hate* him. He has all the qualities I hate most in a bloke. When I saw him wrapped round you last night I wanted to – I dunno. Bury an axe in his skull or something."

"Oh, for God's sake, Maggie—"

"Look. When he turned up again, I told myself I wouldn't interfere. I told myself you had to work it out for yourself, no one could tell you what to do. But I can't *bear* for you to slide back, Coll! You were almost over him – and now he's playing these games with you . . . he's going to *waste* you if you don't watch out."

"Jesus, we only kissed!"

"Yeah – but that's just the start. The beginning. You think you're in control, but you're not."

"One kiss, Maggie. Don't you think you're being a bit paranoid?"

"Yeah, well, I've got good reason to be paranoid, haven't I."

"Have you?

"Yeah. Look – that's sort of why I dragged you in here tonight. I've listened and listened to you, and you said I understood you—"

"You did. You helped me."

"That's because I've been there. All the stuff you told me, all the stuff you were going through – I've been there."

"Why didn't you tell me?"

"Oh God, I didn't want to go dredging it all up again. It's in the past and I've talked it to death. And we were talking about *you*. And it was great, hearing you work it out, pulling yourself up again. But now you're – look. I was with this guy for just over two years, and it was really intense, just like you and Art, and in that time we broke up five times and got back together four times. And I only managed to keep it at four by massive willpower. It *messed me up*. The whole thing messed me up. He was the reason I dropped out of college. And he's the reason I'm applying to different colleges now, so I don't ever have to see him again."

"Oh," I said.

"Yeah, '*oh*'. That shit has taken up *three years* of my life. *Three years* wasted. I don't think about him any more. I'm over him. But what I can't get over is all that waste of *time.* I don't want to see you do that, Coll. I really don't."

There was a long pause, then she said, "Art reminds me of the guy I was with. He's so *sodding sure* of himself. The way he looks at you, as though what he says goes. As though you don't count. As though he can go off and sleep around and then just come back and expect you to want him back. And last night – it was like the way we'd start over again. Just like it. We'd split up, then we'd get off together at a party or something, and it would start up again, and it would be great for a while, and then –"

"What made you split up, all those times?"

"He was abusive," she said abruptly. "Nasty and nice by turns. He used to get really mad, over nothing, and push me around . . . he had a vile temper. It could go on for days, it was insane. I'd try to talk to him and he'd be so *contemptuous. . .* Anyway. I'd crack, I'd break off with him. But then I'd miss him. Because I'd feel so empty without him, because I'd let him take up too much of my life . . . and the sex was – it was just so *brilliant*, it made everything else, every*one* else, seem – you know –"

"Pointless," I said.

"Yes. And then we'd bump into each other and he'd be like this *magnet* – and we'd start up again. And it'd be great for a while – he'd be full of promises about changing. And we'd get all caught up together again, all passionate . . . and he'd start again. Undermining me, bullying me. It was like each time I went back to him, it'd be worse . . . I went right down, Coll. Like I handed all the control to him. I wouldn't wish that on anyone."

"I'm sorry," I said. "I mean – you know. That you went through that."

"Yeah, well, I'm through it now."

"And you're stronger, right? You're a wise woman now."

"Telling you how to live," she laughed.

There was a pause, then I said, "Art isn't abusive. Just – screwed up. I used to feel – you know, I was getting through to him, I was *changing* him –"

"Yeah, well, I thought that too, and it works for a time, and then they revert, and they're pigs again, and your Art – he's an arrogant shit, Coll. You won't change him. You won't."

I fell silent, but I thought: *He's* not *the same. He's not like the guy who messed you up.*

"I can't *bear* it if you slide back like I did, Coll," Maggie was saying. "You should finish it for good. Get out now."

"I know," I said. "Look – nothing'll happen."

"Don't look so miserable. You know what got me? That I felt the most I've ever felt for someone who just . . . kicked it about. But then I worked it out that that didn't make what I felt any less. You know?

What I felt and what you feel now – it was *real*, OK? Most people go through their lives never even touching that kind of feeling. It's special. I'm just going to make sure I pick the right bloke to aim it at next time."

Chapter twenty-five

Whoa. Heavy. That's all I could think as I tramped home.

I went over what Maggie had told me, and I filled in the spaces she wouldn't fill in for me; I tried to imagine her hurt, and weak, and wanting. It was hard. She'd talked about "going down" as if it was descending to some dark, dreadful place, but she'd come up again; she was so strong and together now.

That thought helped me when I got home to find there was no message that Art had phoned. However much I'd told myself he wouldn't, there was still the wraith of a hope inside me that he would. Well, I wasn't going to call him. He was the one who'd left. He was the one who had to come back.

It was Good Friday the next day, and I felt anything but good. I had this feeling I just wanted to get away from it all, escape for a while. Mum was surprised by how compliant I was when she reminded me over the breakfast hot cross buns that we were driving down to the seaside early the next morning, to spend Easter with Auntie Gwen. "What about your shift at the café?" she asked me. "Have you remembered to tell them you want the night off?"

"Yeah," I said. "Don't worry." I'd booked it off ages ago: Bill, the manager, was going to fill in for me.

"Can I ask you to nip out and buy some eggs for the egg hunt?" Mum went on. "I've not had time."

"Oh, *Mum*! Sarah's too old for a stupid egg hunt."

"Don't give me that. Last year you were out there with her, gathering up as many as you could find."

"That's only because I don't *get* any eggs if I don't go out and bloody forage for them. That little sod—"

"Colette – WATCH YOUR LANGUAGE –"

"– She's far too mean to give me as much as a mini-egg, if she's the one that found it. Why can't you just forget the egg hunt, and give me a big bar of choccy, and a wad of notes?"

"Because THAT," said Mum, rising massively to her feet, "is not in the spirit of the Easter festival. We've always had an egg hunt, Colette. Gwen's garden's perfect for it, and she loves to see you children looking through the flowers and—"

"*Mum!*" I wailed. "I'm *seventeen*."

"Oh, so what. You're never too old for some things. Now, here's fifteen pounds. Get lots and LOTS of little ones, OK?"

It was oddly therapeutic, touring the shops, buying up boxes of twee foil-wrapped bunnies and bags full of tiny bright eggs. I even bought a demented-looking fluffy chick, thinking that Sarah might not realize it was inedible, try to bite off its head, and choke. I fixed myself in the present and tried not to think.

We were packed up and off very early the next day. It was nice to just slump like a moron in the back seat of the car, and not have to react to anything. It was nice arriving at Gwen's, and carrying my bag up into the little under-eaves room I always had, with its view of the cliffs and the sea. I shut the door on everyone and opened the window wide. Then I collapsed back on the bed and shut my eyes and listened to the rhythmic soughing of the sea, until I was called down for lunch.

Apart from the family ritual of meals and the gruesome Sunday morning egg hunt and a bit of press-ganged washing up, I was totally free. I divided my time between revision and prowling along the beach and cliffs with Gwen's mad beagle, Tess. Tess would race about rabbiting and I would stalk along, hands in pockets, just letting my thoughts swamp me. *Maybe if I give them free reign*, I thought, *some kind of pattern will emerge.*

It didn't, though. Just the same old confused jumble of need and wanting and regret. My mind only cleared when I stood on the beach and stared at the sea. I'd watch the waves rushing in, then drawing back, fast, rough, and part of me wanted to get in the waves, lose myself in them. The cold wind blowing on my face stopped me, though. The sea had to be much, much colder than the wind; even Tess would barely dip a paw in.

Saturday and Sunday evening, I was so tired I just went to bed early and slept. Deeply, dreamlessly. And I did feel better, stronger, more self-contained, when we drove back on Monday night.

As I helped carry bags into the hall, I noticed the answer machine flashing like a maniac. The whole family gathered round it to hear the messages; it was the first stage of us re-entering our separate lives again. In between the dismal messages from Mum's friends, a business call for Dad from some workaholic who wouldn't even take Easter off, and two Minnie Mouse squeak-alikes for Sarah, there were three for me. One from Joe, sounding cheerful. One from Val, sounding OK. One from Maggie, sounding determined.

Nothing from Art.

Chapter twenty-six

I phoned Val right away, and we chatted about what kind of Easter we'd had. Greg had left a big, glossy Easter egg on the doorstep for her, with a note that said, "Hope you're finding what you want. Still love you."

We spent some time trying to work out from that gift and those nine words whether he most wanted her back, or most wanted her just to be happy. Whether there was a touch of bitterness and regret there, or whether it was just really generous and sweet. Then we came to the unsurprising conclusion that we couldn't know, and anyway, what mattered was that she, Val, was on the right track for herself.

"I've missed him," she said. "I mean – I've felt lonely. Last Saturday was dreadful. But I feel so much less strained, Coll, you know? Like my head's not in a vice any more."

Yeah, I thought, *I know about that vice.*

"So what about you, Coll? How are things for you?"

Tell her, I thought. *Tell her what happened at the concert.*

But I couldn't. I couldn't face her questions, her

disappointment in me. I waffled on about having space and trying to revise, and then Val said how much she wanted to see me so we made a plan to have a day out shopping and stuff on Thursday. It would be another day of putting up a front, but too bad. That was just how it was at the moment. And it was great to feel we were friends again. Val talking to me openly again made me feel more myself, even if I couldn't talk openly back.

I didn't want to phone Joe, in case Art picked up the phone. I went to phone Maggie and discovered I'd lost the bit of paper she'd scribbled her number down on. So I went along to the café the next afternoon instead.

"Hi, sad case," she said cheerfully, as I wandered in. "How's it going? Crawled back to Slime-ball yet?"

"No. Is that why you phoned – to check up on me?"

"Partly. Partly to tell you what I did over Easter."

"Yeah – what?"

"Got off with a French trainee engineer!"

"*Wha-at?*"

"It was brilliant, Coll. He had one of these carved, beautiful faces – and he was *incredibly* fit – and he was all, you know, *wistful* and apologetic 'cos his English was so bad."

"Oh, *wow*, Maggie. Where d'you meet him?"

"A club. I went with some mates, Saturday, after

we closed here. *God* – I just wanted to keep *grabbing* him!"

"So are you going to see him again?"

"Dunno. I asked him for his phone number but he couldn't seem to work out what I was saying. So I gave him mine and he looked completely mystified. Maybe French phone numbers look . different to ours?"

"Not that different. Maybe he's just thick."

"Yeah, probably. I think the language thing could be a problem. Even if he managed to phone me I don't think I'd understand him."

I laughed at her rueful face and she went on, "Never mind, it was great while it lasted. *You* should try it, Coll. Hey – I also wanted to tell you I've got Friday off. All of it. And I thought we could go out somewhere and have a break from this place. We could drive out to the country, go for a walk, and find a pub, and—"

"Drive? I didn't know you'd got a car."

"I've got a motorbike."

I burst out laughing again. "You're kidding!"

"No. Got one as soon as I passed my test, a year ago. I don't bring it to the café 'cos I live so near. I'm really safe on it, Coll – and I've got a spare helmet. Go on, it'll be good for you."

"Well – yeah. Yeah, I'd love to."

"If the weather's good, it'll be brilliant," she said,

pleased. "I know just where we can go."

We agreed a time to meet on Friday, and I left, and as I wandered home I thought about all the effort Val and Maggie, in their different ways, had put into keeping me away from Art. *Girlfriends*, I reflected bleakly, *always seemed to be keener to break you up with someone than get you together.*

Joe rang again, that night. "What is it with you, Coll? You never return calls – you think you're like the Queen or something?"

"Oh, shut up. I was going to phone."

"Yeah, yeah. You'd just better not be busy, that's all. It's my farewell booze-up tomorrow night."

"*Farewell. . .?*"

"Well, OK, not just mine. All the old crowd from school. You know – you met most of them at the party. Holidays are over, Coll. I'm driving back to uni at the weekend."

I felt this rush of panic. "Already?" I didn't want Joe going away.

"Yeah. I want to go back a bit early. There's a house share I might be able to get in on. Anything to get out of my digs. Anyway, Wednesday is the night everyone's free on, so we thought we'd have one last piss-up. You can come, can't you?"

It'll be all his friends, I thought, *that gang from the party – and Art and me.* "Yeah, sure," I said.

Chapter twenty-seven

The next night, heading off to the pub for Joe's farewell drink, I was really wound up. Something in me was ready to smash up that phoney understanding that Art and I were platonic friends. It was like my dream, like keeping a wolf in a cage, putting your arms through, letting it lick you, saying I'm safe, I'm safe, it's shut in there. And all the time you're just waiting for that cage door to open, for the bars to break.

Last Wednesday, after the gig, they'd broken. And yet we were carrying on as if they hadn't. I was fed up with it. I had the strongest need just to talk straight. *Be* straight.

There were about twelve people there when I got to the pub, mostly grouped untidily round the bar. I saw Art immediately, noted who he was standing next to, saw he wasn't really talking to anyone, or smiling. He was like a black hole, taking all my attention. Joe greeted me happily, and asked me what I wanted to drink. Art gave me a half smile and a nod, eyes hooded. It was like we were both waiting.

After we'd half emptied our glasses and chatted and joked for a while – I was loud, Art almost silent –

a large table at the side of the pub cleared. It was next to a smaller, emptier one, and everyone made a scramble for them. There were just enough chairs to go round. Fake Elizabethan panelling, curving round us into a type of booth, helped the intimate atmosphere.

Art and I had gravitated speechlessly together. I was sitting at the smaller table, on the bench against the wall, next to one of Joe's old school friends. Art was on the other side of him, at the end of the table. Joe and a couple of others seized the dog-eared card menus that were lying on the table and started discussing how hungry they were and whether they should fork out for chicken and chips. And I took in a deep breath, then I leaned behind the bloke next to me and asked Art how his hod carrying was going.

He smiled, but didn't look at me. "It's not just hod carrying. It's all right. Boring. Pays well, though."

We talked aimlessly for a while; the point was just to be in conversation, it didn't matter what we said. We looked round at each other more and more; then we twisted to face each other. Art asked me if I wanted another drink, and I said yes please. He stood up and went to the bar, and came back with a drink for me, one for himself, and one for Joe. There were far too many people there to buy a round for everyone.

"What about college?" I asked. "Did you get it fixed up?"

"Yeah, I think so. I –" He broke off. The guy between us was leaning across Art, talking loudly to a girl on the other side of the table. "Hey, mate," Art said, "You want to trade places?" The guy stood up and shuffled round Art, still continuing to talk loudly. And Art took his place next to me.

It was like moves in a chess game. First buy me a drink, then take the seat next to me. Under the table, his leg was almost touching mine. He started telling me about the college course he was going for, then he suddenly stopped, looked at me, smiled, not very pleasantly, and said, "How's Maggie?"

"Fine," I shrugged. "Why?"

"No reason. She looked like poison the other night. She saw us together, didn't she. After the gig. She saw us kissing."

I shrugged, and turned away, to cover the fact that I'd gone red.

"Why d'you hang around with her?" he went on. "Don't you see enough of her at the café?"

"There's not much chance to talk at the café. And I like her."

"Yeah? I don't."

"Well that's fine," I said, with satisfaction, "because she can't *stand* you."

"Yeah? What's she said? Don't bother, I can guess. Warning you off, right?"

"Something like that."

"Sodding man-hater. What would she know."

I twisted round in my seat and glared at him. "Manhater? Just 'cos she didn't take to *you*?"

"She's a dyke, isn't she?"

"*God* you –" I took in a breath. "No, she isn't. She's a friend. And it's *normal* to have friends, Art. I know you're not too good at it, and you tend to lose friends 'cos you do stuff like sleep with their girlfriends, but believe me, it's normal."

He grinned. "OK, don't get all stressed."

"And she's got nothing to do with you."

"OK, OK. It just *interests* me, that's all. You know – what kind of scene you're getting into."

"Yeah? What about the *scene* you've been into, while you were away?"

He shrugged.

"Maybe *I'm* interested in that," I went on. "Maybe *I'm* interested in you shagging your way round New Zealand." Just at this point there was a lull in the general conversation, and everyone heard me, and they all turned to stare at Art.

"That's my business," he muttered.

"Yeah? Well, Maggie's mine."

Art glowered over at Joe, who got very involved in finishing his pint. "What else has he been telling you?"

"Oh, about Maria. The older woman."

Almost despite himself, a sort of pleased smirk

invaded Art's features. "Yeah? What's he said about her?"

"Oh – that she picked you up, and you're now a card-carrying member of the Union of Gigolos."

"Yeah, right."

"Seriously, Art – how much did she pay you? By the night?"

"By the orgasm. I'm a millionaire now, kid."

I wanted to attack him when he said that, a real, talon-flying attack, but I resisted it. I put everything into looking amused and a bit indifferent. "What was she like?" I asked.

"Oh, all right," he said. "Glamorous. Took forever to get ready. Stacks of clothes and stuff."

"Was she – I mean, did you *talk*?"

"She didn't exactly pick me up to chat, Coll."

"Oh, shut up. You know what I mean."

"No, we didn't talk much. Just – surface stuff."

This was half killing me, this interrogation, pretending to be flip and cool, but I had to know, I had to. "So what did you do apart from screw each other?" I blurted out.

Art linked his hands behind his neck and stretched backwards, with the beginning of a grin. "Um. What did we do. Lots of lazing on the beach, lots of travelling, stayed at expensive places – saunas, jacuzzis, the whole corny bit. I got good at massages. Even foot massages."

"Oh, throw *up*."

He turned to me. "You want one?"

"*No*."

"Maria liked – she liked the good life. She liked spending money. Good wine, good food. . ."

"No wonder you didn't talk much. You don't know how an egg gets cooked."

"Ah, she talked to the waiters about all that, not me. Big discussions before she'd order anything."

"And didn't you feel a bit of a *jerk*?" I almost exploded. "Sitting there while she whacked on about the wine menu? And never being the one to pay the bill?"

There was a pause, and then Art said, "Yeah, sometimes. There was one night I was really pissed off. I just wanted to get out on my own, but I knew I couldn't, not without a fight. Then when we were walking out of the restaurant I looked through the glass doors into the kitchen, and saw these two guys my age – one was washing up and one was peeling spuds."

"And you thought, I could be doing their job – they could be doing mine?"

"No, they were too ugly to be me."

"Yeah, right."

"But it did make me think."

"That it was a job."

"Yeah."

"You felt ashamed."

"Jesus, Coll, I never realized what a Puritan you are. I didn't feel *ashamed*. A lot of the time I felt pretty good, if you want the truth. I didn't feel like it was *me* being exploited."

"Yeah, but – you did see it as a job."

He shrugged. "Well, she was the one with the money. Which meant she had the power. I was sleeping in her hotel room, adding to her restaurant bills, travelling in her car – it was weird. It bothered her a lot more than me. She'd keep getting into these discussions, justifying it, saying her old man had a mistress and spent stacks of money on her, so why shouldn't she have fun for once. She got a real kick out of just *watching* me. She'd sit at the edge of the pool and watch me swim, and—"

"I don't want to hear."

"OK."

"What did she look like?"

"About your height. Very curvy. Huge tits. Black, curly hair. Half Spanish or something. Lazy. Never got in the pool with me."

"And what was . . . what was. . ." But I couldn't say it, I couldn't ask what it had been like, going to bed with her. "Why did it finish?"

"She went back to her husband. Back to reality, she reckoned. So I was out on my own again, and very poor – and that's when I came home."

There was a long silence. "You're fuming, Coll," he said.

"Yeah, well. I think it's *revolting*. I'd never do that, I'd never just sleep with someone just to—"

"It's a bit different."

"No it isn't. It's called being a prostitute whatever sex you are."

He pulled a face at me. "Look. Her money wasn't the only reason I went off with her. It just –"

"Helped."

"Yeah, well. I'm not very good at doing without money."

"Not used to it, you mean."

"Maybe. When my money ran out I got sick of hitch-hiking and sleeping on the beach and never having a hot shower and eating cheap crap. She came along just when I really wanted to get out."

I fixed him with a stony expression.

"Oh, Coll, stop looking so bloody superior," he snapped. "At least I stick to the opposite sex."

"*What*?"

"You heard."

"Oh, *Jesus*, Art, I've told you, Maggie and I are *friends*. Is that too weird for you?"

"Whenever I see you two you're joined at the hip."

I stared at him, speechless, for a couple of seconds, and then I realized he was jealous. I let this fact sink into me like honey into bread.

"I like her," I said. "I like her a lot. And I don't see why it bothers you."

"It doesn't bother me."

"So why are you going on about it?"

There was a long pause. I shifted in my seat. We'd suddenly got so intimate it was overpowering. "Anyway," I went on. "Is she – Maria – is she the stuff you needed to talk about? You said a lot of stuff happened to you in New Zealand, stuff you needed to talk about –"

"Did I?"

"Yeah – you know. In your letter." Then I blushed, because I realized I made it sound as though I knew his letter off by heart. Which I did, of course, but I didn't want him to know that.

"Oh – right. Yeah, partly. And not being in touch with the old man for like, months – him not knowing where I was. I began to think it wasn't such a bad way to live. I was – I was wondering whether to make it permanent, just not get in touch again. Only when I got back to England I was flat broke, I had nowhere to stay, so I just turned up. He was so livid with me he practically beat me up, then we made up, but then . . . within a week we were at each other's throats again."

"Why?" I said quietly. "What over?"

"Oh, everything. We can't get on. We can't forgive each other."

187

"Forgive each other? What –"

"Coll, let's just drop it, OK?"

"I'll get another round," I said, beginning to stand, but Art stood up too, put a hand on my shoulder, and pushed me back down.

"No, I'll get it. I'm loaded, remember? For once."

I smiled up at him. "Yeah, with your own money. *For once.*" He grinned then and suddenly sat back down again, turning right towards me. "It feels great, Coll. Even though it's a bonehead job, it feels great, to have your own cash, not to have to jump through hoops to – Dad always made it clear I did what he wanted or I didn't get a penny."

"What about Maria – she do that too?"

"Oh, shut up. What scares me now is this college thing – Dad wants to approve the course, he wants this heavy business course – I want to do something with marine biology. He won't even discuss it with me. There's this ocean studies course I'd love to do. Marine biology, navigation, everything. Not sure if my maths is up to it, but if it *is –*"

I looked at his face, all vibrant with wanting, and purpose, and I thought, *Oh shit, no. The last thing I want to feel for you is – a new kind of attraction.*

"It was the sea in New Zealand that got me fixed on it," he said. "I'd love to study it – I just want to go *back* there." He leaned towards me, said, "You'd love it, Coll," then he stood up again and loped off to the bar, and I sat dazed. My shoulder still felt warm from the pressure of his hand.

Chapter twenty-eight

Art bought the drinks just as last orders was being called, and when he sat down again beside me it was clear that the time of intimacy was over. I think it had shaken both of us, that closeness, that return to how we used to be. I turned to the rest of the table and tried to make small talk but inside I felt confused, scared, awkward.

Then there was a sudden burst of boozy farewell toasts to Joe and all the others who were going back, and the conversation round the table turned general, with everyone moaning about the Easter holidays coming to an end too soon. The barmen began gathering up glasses noisily; it was time to leave. We all stood up, bundling on coats. Joe collared me as I made my way out from behind the table. "I've hardly spoken to you," he said meaningfully. "You all right?"

"I dunno," I whispered.

He put his arms round me and gave me a big bear squeeze. "I'm not off till Sunday morning. Maybe I'll drop by and say goodbye before then, yeah?"

"Oh, Joe – that'd be great."

As we all made our way to the door, Art drew up beside me. "Bye, Coll," he said, with the ghost of a shrug. "It's been good just – you know – talking."

Just talking, I thought. *That wasn't* just talking, *you idiot. I'm charged when I speak to you, every part of me. Your imprint is all over me – like mine is on you.*

I can't bear it. I don't know what we're going to do.

It was quite a relief to meet Val the next day, and wander down to the shopping centre. Without actually agreeing to, we avoided all serious topics of talk and spent the first few hours like real girlies, talking about tops and nail varnishes and how much we'd be prepared to spend on a bra. Then we got hungry and Val said we should treat ourselves and have a real ladies-who-lunch lunch, so we went into a little pasta place instead of the usual sarnies from M&S or a burger.

We ordered a glass of white wine each, and pasta and a green salad to share, and enjoyed the waiter flirting with us, and the sense of occasion. When the food arrived I watched Val as she twirled spaghetti inexpertly on her fork, and I felt this huge urge to spill everything out to her. But I knew it would have been a disaster. It would have meant going too far back, explaining too much; it would have been asking too much of her. And anyway, she had her own stuff to tell.

"Greg phoned up last night," she said. "We had

this kind of agreement we'd get in touch after Easter, so –"

"Yeah? What'd he say?"

"Dunno. Wouldn't speak to him."

"Blimey. That's a bit heavy, Val."

"I know. Mum called up the stairs, and I – I just acted from the gut. I just felt *no*! So I told Mum to say I was in the shower. Only then I didn't phone him back. I still haven't. I just – I really don't want to. I've felt so good, this last week. I mean it's been like this weight going. I've felt *normal*. It's like – if I speak to him, I'll go back to how I was, or something."

"Did he phone again?"

"No. Well, it was quite late. But he didn't phone this morning. Actually – I got out of the house early. I just don't want to face it. It's not *him*. It's what we had together, all that crap – how *I* was. I just want to leave it behind."

"You mean that? Like – for good?"

Val looked at me. "I think so. Yeah, I do. I mean – it's scary just to say, that's it, finish. But the thought of going back is scarier. If you know what I mean."

We wound up at a cinema, seeing a third-rate action movie that gave us a lot of laughs in all the wrong places. Then we wandered back to my place. Mum was beside herself with pleasure at seeing Val again; it made me realize just how long it had been since we'd acted like ordinary friends. She insisted on reheating us some dodgy-looking stew that we were too hungry to refuse, then she started making noises about Val being welcome to stay the night, no trouble to make up a bed etc. etc. I knew I had to get off early the next day to meet Maggie, though, so I didn't push it, and Val ended up phoning for a taxi at about eleven o'clock.

"D'you think I *should* phone Greg?" she said, as we stood outside, to wait for the cab.

"I dunno. It seems a bit mean just to leave him hanging. But if you hate the thought of it *that* much. . ."

"Maybe I'll write again. Maybe I'll write and say – I'll see you to talk if you really want to, but I'm sorting myself out better, on my own . . . you know, Coll, I bet he'd be relieved. If I did that."

"Maybe. I know how much he cares for you, though, and how –"

"Guilty he feels."

"Yeah, well. That, too."

"He'd be relieved, I know he would."

A cab drew up beside us, and a man leaned out and said, "Miss Sparks?"

"Thanks," called Val. Then she turned to me, and we put our arms round each other and hugged. "It's been great, today, Coll."

"Yeah," I said. "Take it easy. Give me a ring soon. Let me know what you decide."

Chapter twenty-nine

Maggie had warned me to wear gear to walk in for our day out on Friday, and told me to put on something tough – "just in case you come off the bike – not that you will, I promise – but just in case." So I got up early the next day and rooted through the understairs cupboard, looking for Dad's old brown leather flying jacket. He'd given up wearing it because Mum always made sneering comments about attempts to recapture lost youth when he did, but I knew he'd refused to give it away.

I found the jacket, and escaped upstairs to check the look of it in my mirror. It was big on me, but it looked OK. With my hair pulled back in a pony tail and my old DMs and jeans, I looked like a biker. Which was OK, because that was what I was going to be for a day.

I managed to grab breakfast and find some old leather gloves and get out of the house before Mum questioned my outfit. She didn't approve of motorbikes.

I was outside the café well by ten to meet Maggie, like we'd arranged. I couldn't help giggling as this gleaming machine roared round the corner and came to a halt beside me. It seemed so incongruous, somehow. Maggie climbed off and pulled off her helmet. She had a full set of leathers on, and her hair was in wild little spikes round her head.

"OK, what's so funny?" she said, grinning.

"You! You're like something out of *Mad Max*!"

"Yeah? Cool. You look like someone out of a World War II flying movie. Come on, here's your helmet. Let's get going."

As I struggled with the helmet strap under my chin, I eyed the bike a bit nervously. "It's big, isn't it?"

"No. Standard."

"I've never been on one before."

"Coll – stop acting so chicken! I won't do a ton till you're used to the feel."

She swung back on, and I climbed up awkwardly behind her. "Now – put your arms round my waist, and move when I do, OK?" she said. "Just go with the movement of the bike." Then she kicked it into life, and we rode slowly away down the road.

"OK?" she yelled back over her shoulder.

"Yeah!" I shouted, holding on a bit tighter. It was like being on my bike, only faster, and effortless. It was thrilling.

"Sure?"

"Yeah! It's great!"

Maggie took this as a cue to speed up, and soon we'd left the town behind us, and were out into open roads. I could feel my ponytail streaming out behind me and my eyes blurred from watching everything rip past us but I felt surprisingly safe.

"Getting greener!" Maggie yelled back at me. The roads got narrower and more winding as we headed through fields and woodlands. Then suddenly Maggie pulled over into a little lay-by at the side of the road, and turned round. She was laughing. "Coll, I'm not doing any steering!"

"What?"

"I know I said move with the bike, but you're moving so much you're turning into the corners before I do!"

"Oh. Sorry."

"Just move *with* me, OK? Relax."

She kicked the bike into motion once more, and after another fifteen minutes, we'd arrived at a little country pub. "If we lock the bike up here," she said, "we can go for a mooch around, and then get back here for lunch, yeah? They've got a good cook here. I used to work for her."

"Sounds great," I said. I waited while she peeled her leather trousers off – she had thin jeans on underneath. She opened the trunk thing on the back of the bike, bundled in the trousers, and took out a bottle of lemonade. We both had a swig of this, then she chained up the bike and we headed off across the road, on to a little signposted country lane.

I felt exhilarated after the bike ride. The sun was beginning to get really warm, and everything seemed fresh and open. We talked for a bit about when Maggie had worked at the pub, and how long she'd had the bike, and then I asked how her college applications were going.

"They've gone," she said, with some satisfaction. "I've just heard I've got a place at Portsmouth, doing textiles and design."

"Maggie, that is great news!" I crowed, stopping in my tracks. "Congratulations! Why didn't you tell me?"

"I'm telling you now!"

I laughed, and hugged her, and we carried on walking. "I haven't actually accepted the place yet," she went on. "It's scary stuff, going to a new college, especially when you made such a cock-up of the last one. And it's a long way from home."

"But you're going to accept, aren't you?" I said.

"Yes. Yes, of course I am. This September, I'm making a new start."

We left the little lane and walked out on to a sloping field with a great, curved horizon. It felt weird, knowing Maggie was off in September, knowing this friendship we'd made was just for a time. But there was something exhilarating about that too. The point of it was here, now.

I smiled, and quickened my pace a bit, and Maggie matched me.

"What about you, Coll?" Maggie said. "What are your plans for after the exams?"

"*After* the exams? I'm not thinking about after them. That's like life after death – I'm not sure it exists."

"It exists," she laughed. "You taking a year off?"

"I think so. God, Maggie, I don't know. I haven't thought. It's just been work and –"

"Dealing with the return of Gitface."

"Yeah."

"Well, you should do it. Do something good. Get out of here. I wish I'd taken a year off. I wish I'd travelled. Not wasted all that time on that *loser*."

We fell silent after that and just walked. The sun was really hot now. I found myself remembering all the times I'd been out in the country with Art, the way we'd walk, and talk, and look for somewhere hidden to make love.

"I love this," said Maggie, dreamily. "I love being out in the open. What are you thinking about?"

"Oh, nothing."

"Gitface, I bet. Having sex in a haystack with him."

I burst out laughing. "We *never* did it in a haystack. Too spiky."

"H'mm. Have you seen him again?"

"Yeah," I said, reluctantly. "Last night. There was a whole crowd of us, and. . ."

"He just merged into the background, right?"

"Well. . ."

"OK, OK. Your business. Come on, let's make it to the top of that hill. We can have a breather. Finish off the lemonade."

We got to the top and sat down with our backs against an old fallen tree trunk, taking turns to swig from the lemonade bottle. I stared out towards the horizon, then I said, "You're not right about Art, you know. I mean – I know he seems arrogant and stuff, but that's his front. Underneath he's not. I mean – once he's worked through all the crap and sorted out things with his dad and grown out of this thing he has about going from girl to girl he's –"

"Going to be great. Yeah, Coll, he will. He'll also be about thirty-five years old."

"Oh, shut up," I said. We were both laughing.

"Look, if he'd come back and told you what an idiot he'd been and said he wanted you back or he just wanted to be friends you'd have had – I dunno, something to go on. But he's just *messing* with you. Even if he doesn't mean to. You've got this big attraction there still, this big sex thing – and yet no one's admitting it, and . . . it's just not *honest*."

"I know."

"And I know how much you're drawn to him still. It's just – how long is it going to go on for? I reckon you've served your term, you know? You should be allowed out."

I stood up, and stretched out my arms above my head, easing my shoulders. "Let's get going," I said. "Let's go back and get some lunch. I'm *starving*."

We headed back down the hill, down into the pub, and ordered an enormous lunch and giggled all the way through it. I felt reckless, free of something; we talked about what we wanted to do in the future, the travelling we wanted to do, all the different things we wanted to experience. After lunch we rode off to a nearby market town and stooged about for a bit, then we came home. Maggie dropped me off at the end of my road and I gave her her helmet back.

"Thanks," I said. "It's been a great day."

And it had been. A great, free, wonderful day, like days ought to be. Maggie smiled, waved, roared off, and I headed into the house. I had something to do.

Chapter thirty

"Art? Hi, it's me."

"Coll. Hi."

"I need to speak to you."

"Speak."

"No, I mean I – I want to talk to you. Can we meet? Are you busy tonight?"

"No."

"Well, can we –" *Help me out, you bastard.* "Can we –"

"You could come here. Joe's being taken out by his folks – farewell meal."

"Oh – OK. Yeah. What time?"

"They're going out at seven thirty."

"Right. See you then." And I put the phone down.

It was nearly six o'clock. I got showered and changed and made up, blocking out the little voice asking me why I wanted to look so good for him. Then I got a cab round to Joe's place, marched straight up to the front door, and knocked.

I didn't dare pause, in case I lost my nerve.

Art opened it, unsmiling. His hair was still wet, spiky, from the shower; he was barefoot, with jeans and a white shirt on, wide open at the neck. "Hi," he said.

"Hi. Have they gone?"

"Yeah. Come in." I followed him in to the hall. "What's this about, Coll?"

"I told you, I need to talk to you."

"OK. Want a beer?"

I followed him into the kitchen, and he pulled a couple of bottles out of the fridge and chinked the tops off on the side of the table. "Here."

"Thanks."

We both took a long pull, then he said, "Well, you want to go out, or what? Or talk here?"

I looked around me, at the big family kitchen. It felt open, echoing.

"Go up to my room if you like," he said.

I wasn't sure that this was a good idea, but I found myself nodding. He walked out into the hall and up the stairs and I trooped out after him.

He'd been given one of Joe's sisters' rooms. It was square, cosy. There was some sort of wavy blue paintwork on the walls, a bit like the sea, and a soft red blind at the window. I headed for the one chair in the room and sat down on it. Art subsided on to the edge of the bed and took another long swig of beer "So," he said. "Talk to me, Coll."

"OK." I took in a long, shuddery breath. "Look. This being friends, it's not working for me, Art."

"What d'you mean?"

"I mean – it's been good to see you again and everything. And – you know – find out you're all right. But well, Joe's going back to college, and I don't think . . . I don't think we should see each other once he's gone."

"Joe. What's he got to do with it? I didn't see you talking to him much last night."

"No. Well."

"I thought *we* got on OK."

"Yeah. We did. It's just – look, I thought I'd get used to it, but I haven't. I can't think of you as a friend, Art, I just can't."

He shrugged. "So what do you think of me as?"

I could feel myself being backed into a corner, and I hated it. "It's just – you know. It was a really intense time, when we were together, and –"

"Yeah, it was. For me, too. But just because you've slept with someone doesn't mean you –"

"Look, I can't just switch off."

"Who's asking you to?"

"Oh, for *Christ's* sake, you're not listening to me." I could feel my throat tightening, tears coming. "Look – I can't cope with it, OK? I can't get that sort of distance. I can't be casual – not like you. That time after the gig, when we got off together. . ."

"Yeah?"

"I can't just *do* that, Art, I can't. Not like it's – *nothing*."

"It wasn't nothing, Coll. It was great."

"Oh – *look*." I felt this warmth flood into me, when he said that. "I need to stay away, all right? I mean I – it's screwing me up. I *hated* hearing about all the women you got through in New Zealand."

"So why did you ask me about them?"

"Oh *Jesus*! Because I was curious, of course I was curious. But I can't be – it still *hurts*. I mean – yeah, we're over, we're finished, but I need that to be final, you know? I don't want it all stirred up again – every time I see you."

There was a long pause. Art stood up and walked over to the window and stood looking out at the garden

"Why not?" he said.

I gawped at him. "Because I can't *deal* with it, that's why! You might be able to take it in your stride, but I *can't*. Oh Jesus." I stood up, headed for the door. "This is useless. I'm going." I reached for the handle but before I could grab it Art had crossed the room and slammed his hand on the door. "Don't go, Coll," he said. "Please. Let's sort this out."

He was about a hand's width away from me now. My throat had closed up so tight it ached. I shut my eyes, and said, "There's nothing *to* sort out. It screws me up too much to see you, that's all. I want to . . . I want to move on."

I could feel his face near mine. I could hear him

breathing. I didn't dare open my eyes. "Why? Why d'you want to move on?"

I opened my eyes, looked straight into his. "You've moved on," I said.

"Jesus, Coll, stop trying to live your life in a straight line. Yeah, I've moved on, but I still want to see you. I like your company. I like talking to you. Why d'you have to be such a drama queen about everything?"

"Get away from the door, Art," I muttered. I felt as though I was going to break down any minute. "Please."

He didn't move. "Is this Maggie's advice?" he sneered.

"What?"

"Your *friend*. She been telling you to cut old ties?"

I didn't answer. He leaned closer. "I hate that cow. Why can't she stay out of it?"

"Stay out of what?"

"Out of other people's lives. *My* life."

"She's not in your life."

"She is. She's in my face the whole time. She's always with you. And this is her, isn't it?" He took his hand from the door and got hold of my arm with it. "She's put you up to it. Hasn't she? *Hasn't she?*"

I could have stopped him, pulled away, at any time, but I didn't. I breathed in the smell of beer on his breath as his mouth got closer and closer. "This has got nothing to do with Maggie," I muttered. "It's me."

"Oh, come on, Coll," he said, and then he sort of jerked me, so that I stumbled forward. We collided, body to body; his face crashed against mine.

And then we were kissing, grabbing for each other. And the width of his shoulders under my arms was right, so right I felt half crazy with it; I slid my hands inside his shirt and ran them along and felt his skin, his bones; I reached for his hair, I pulled his head down towards me, slid my fingers down the muscles on his neck. It was so right I could have wept. The cage was unlocked, it was broken; all I wanted was to be locked together.

He got hold of the waistband of my jeans while we were still kissing and started twisting the buttons open. I stretched up; I made it easier. Then somehow we shed what clothes we had to, and made it over to the bed, and he fell on top of me. I wound my legs round his and we carried on kissing and biting and then one-handedly he fumbled on a Durex and pushed inside me. I heard myself groan, and I moved closer, and closer, and then he was saying "Oh God, Coll, I'm sorry, I'm sorry, it'll be better next time."

Chapter thirty-one

There was a great, empty pause, then Art shunted off me and turned away to get rid of the condom. I muttered, "Oh God, suppose they come back or something," then I slid off the bed and started pulling my clothes on. I couldn't look at him. I could feel this great hollow space begin to spread inside my stomach.

"Coll, I'm sorry," he said. "I was too quick."

I didn't reply. I was stooped over my boots, zipping them up.

"I guess it was the shock," he said, and then he laughed, as though he hoped I might join in.

I picked up my bag and headed for the door. "I've got to go," I croaked, then I clattered down the stairs so loudly that if he made a reply, I didn't hear it.

I slammed the front door and raced along the road, heading for the taxi rank at the edge of town. I recognized the state of being I was in – I'd been there before. I was all energy, clear thinking. I had to act before I got muddled and muddied again, before all the hurt crashed in and swamped me like a tidal wave. I went straight home and ran upstairs, sat at my desk and wrote to him.

Art

I didn't mean that to happen, but at least it proves my point – that we can't go on seeing each other as "friends". Maybe you think it's fine for us to have sex like that – for old times' sake, just because we used to, but I can't be like that – I don't want to be like that. Maybe I'm just naïve. You're the only person I've ever slept with. I can't just move on to the next person, like you can. I've hardly ever *kissed* anyone since we split up. You know what you meant to me – what you still mean – you must do. Now I want to get over it, but I can't just turn you off like a light switch. It was a mistake to see you again.

My exams are very soon. I don't want you to phone me, or call me – I don't want to see you.

Please, Art.

Coll

I read it through once and made no changes. Then I ran out of the house and posted it at the pillarbox on the corner of our road, and ran home again. In the kitchen, I opened one of Mum's bottles of wine and poured myself out a huge beakerful and took it upstairs. I slumped down on my bed and lay there, propped on one elbow, drinking determinedly.

I was lost in how hollow it had been when we'd made love. Had sex, rather. Isolated sex – sex in a vacuum. What had overtaken me so desperately when we'd started to kiss had been some kind of frantic nostalgia, nostalgia for how it used to be between us. I couldn't get that back – just the act. Just the ghost of the act.

It wasn't anything to do with the sex being hurried, over too fast. I felt like we could have been there for hours, made love ten more times, and I still wouldn't have come, and I'd still feel this empty. Like a plant without roots, it couldn't flourish.

My skylight went from grey to black as I lay there on my bed. I finished the wine and at around ten thirty I slipped downstairs to make myself a cup of coffee. The tidal wave I'd been expecting, the great crash of emotion – it hadn't come. I had no desire, no need, to talk to anyone.

I've never read or seen or heard anything where sleeping with someone after you've split up with them isn't meant to be a bad thing. It's giving in, sliding back, letting go; it's opening old wounds, rekindling desires, and God knows how many other cliches all rolled into one. Well, all I can say is, I didn't regret it. I felt like something had come to an end, like a door had slammed shut inside me. I'd gone round intending to tell him we had to stop seeing each other – and that's what I'd done.

The next day when I woke up I felt empty, free. The one thing I regretted was posting the letter, not getting it hand-delivered somehow. It wouldn't reach Art till Monday, and I couldn't feel safe until he read it.

I phoned Maggie and told her I couldn't make it to the café that night. Then I told her what had happened – just the facts – and said I wanted to hide until Art got my letter. I couldn't risk him coming round to the café. She told me fine, and said she was proud of me, making that decision, and I said I'd see her soon, and rang off.

I felt safe at home. I didn't think Art would try and come round there and if he did, Mum could field him.

I got my exam timetable out and sellotaped it to the wall. And I worked like a fury all day. I kept waiting for the energy to die on me, for some kind of regret or misery to swamp me, but it didn't. I took a couple of hours off at lunchtime, when I made myself a sandwich and went for a bike ride. I still felt no need to speak to anyone.

At nine thirty in the evening the door bell went, and so did my composure. I waited with baited breath, hanging down from my hatch, to see if it was Art.

"COLETTE! Somebody to see you!" It wasn't Art, it couldn't be. Mum sounded far too pleasant.

I couldn't tell if the pounding in my chest was

relief or disappointment as I hurried down the stairs. It was Joe, standing in the hall.

"Hi," he said, warmly. "I said I'd come and see you before I left. I called in at the café, and Maggie said you were ill." He craned forward to look at me. "You do look weird, Coll. You all right?"

"Yes. Yeah, I'm not ill. Just – I needed a night off."

"Right off? Or can you come out for one last little drink? I've done all my packing. I've got the car outside."

I smiled. "I'd love to, Joe."

We went to a nearby pub where the lights were too bright and the music was crap, but it didn't matter, it was only for one drink. On the way there, in the car, I pledged to myself that I wouldn't ask one question about Art, but I didn't really need to make the pledge. I didn't want to talk about it.

We chatted, calmly, quietly, knowing the holidays were really over now, knowing the next stage was on us. He told me not to get too hyper about the exams; I told him to get his courage up and ask out the angel in his politics group. Then he drove me back home.

Before I got out of the car, I said, "Joe, you've been great these holidays. You really have. I'm going to miss you."

"I'll write to you."

"You will?"

"Yeah, Coll." He pulled my hair back from my

face, smiling at me. "I always like the wrong girls. If you hadn't been Art's ex – I'd have asked you out, you know."

"Joe, you did ask me out. Lots of times. We're out now."

"No dummy. I mean ask-you-out. As in date. As in snog at the end of it."

I smiled, and leaned my forehead against his. "Yeah, Joe. I know."

And then somehow, his face had twisted down towards mine, and his mouth had found mine.

When Art kissed you, his hands were always part of it. Pulling me into him, pulling me close. Art's kisses were just the start, the preliminary to what really mattered, and the better the kiss, the sooner his hands came round, on my neck, on my breasts. . . But this was a kiss with just our mouths touching. It was suspended, isolated, erotic. There was nowhere for it to go, so it just improved on itself. It got better, and better, like a conversation, like real communication.

Until finally, I pulled away, as gently as I could.

"Blimey," breathed Joe.

"Yeah. Blimey."

"I didn't think I could kiss like that."

"Well you can. Evidently."

He grinned at me, and I said, "I'd better go, Joe."

"Yeah," he said. "I'll write to you, Coll."

Chapter thirty-two

I went at my exams like someone digging herself a shelter before the bomb bursts. Whatever happened, I had to get them. They were my passport, my escape, my ticket out. I lived quietly, except I saw Val quite a bit; we'd revise together, keep each other going. She'd been to two sessions at the clinic and said it had helped her; she'd met Greg for a drink once, but that had been all.

I never did tell her about what happened with Art. There was no need to now. Sometimes I'd find myself remembering him, but I could set him aside far more easily than before.

I'd stopped working at the café when the exam countdown started, but Maggie would phone me up occasionally and we'd go out on her bike or to a club and have a fantastic time. Joe wrote to me twice, and I wrote back; he still hadn't plucked up courage to ask the angel out, but he had his sights on someone in his philosophy group now. We never mentioned the kiss we'd had; it would have been too – complicated, taking it further. Maggie's bike rides, Joe's kiss – they were like signs on the road going out, like glimpses of what life could be.

I won't go on about the exams. Together they formed a long, dark tunnel which I just about managed to crawl through and come out the other end. And then, perversely, I felt deflated when they were over. Sure, we all went out to celebrate, and the relief was like something you could throw your head back and drink in great draughts, but I felt shiftless. There'd been so much going on for me just before exams started that I hadn't given a thought to what I wanted to do afterwards. And yet everyone else seemed to know what they were doing.

Rachel and Caro were working in France for a bit because they were going on to study French. Val was going straight off to Sheffield University; Greg was going to work for a bit, and then travel with one of his mates. Then he wasn't following her to Sheffield. They'd agreed to be friends, but they seemed to need to keep away from each other. The damage had gone deep.

And Maggie was off too, of course. College Take Two, as she called it. She'd got into a great-sounding house share a ten-minute bike ride from the college. She told me I could come and stay and I said that would be great in the vague way you do when you're not sure what you'll be doing in two months' time.

There's only so long you can tell yourself you're going to wait until the results come out before you decide what you're going to do in the future. I'd had a generous offer from York University, and my coursework grades were OK, so unless I'd had a real brainstorm during the papers and written gobbledegook instead of the answers I thought I'd done, I sort of knew I'd get through. I had an option on a gap year, and I wanted to take it. I was stumped though. I had no plans, no ideas. And no one rootless like me to discuss it with.

Mum and I had loads of rows about it. Her attitude seemed to be that if I couldn't think of something I wanted to do with the year, I should get straight to university. I could see her point, but she didn't understand the need I had just to *drift* for a while. Somewhere deep inside, I felt exhausted.

One morning over toast and marmalade Mum was lecturing me about how action shakes off depression when Sarah brought in two letters for her. She read the top envelope and her face went all sort of clayey – kind of pale and collapsed. "Oh God," she said. "Oh no. Not this summer. Oh NO."

"What is it, Mum?"

"Oh God. It's Auntie Grace. I bet she – yes she does. She wants to visit. Oh God. Her last time, she says. It was her last time last time. Only it wasn't. Obviously."

"Mum, you're raving. Who's Auntie Grace?"

"Don't you remember? You must have been –

what, eight, nine? She came to stay. For three long weeks."

I frowned. "I can't – she's not the one who lives in Canada, is she?"

"Yes. She must be over seventy now. My only remaining aunt. Oh GOD!"

I'd started to laugh. It was quite a treat to see Mum so ruffled. "Mum, what's the *problem*?"

"Oh, nothing. Only I'll have to clear out of my office and make it into a spare room for her. And we'll have to eat meat all the time because she has this grisly idea that she's got to have something on her plate that's 'drawn breath'. And she says don't worry about me, I'm independent, but then she goes off and gets herself into TROUBLE. She got lost for four hours up in town last visit – we found her wandering round Soho, peering into all the sex show windows . . . oh GOD. And I've got a really busy time on at work, too."

Then Mum looked at me.

"Don't even think about it, Mum," I said.

"Oh, come on, you were saying only just now you were in a limbo. You don't have to do MUCH with her. Just a couple of shows in town – an art gallery or so. She says she comes to England for the culture. She likes Lloyd Webber, God help us."

"Yeah, well I'm not sitting through *Cats* again."

"Colette, you loved it!"

"I was *twelve* when I loved it!"

"Come on, help me out."

"When's she coming?"

Mum checked the letter again and let out a groan. "The end of next week."

Chapter thirty-three

Well, at least the impending visit was a distraction. I booked up for a couple of musicals on the firm understanding that I'd only have to accompany Auntie Grace to one, and I helped Mum clear out her office and turn it back into a bedroom again. "I'll have to move this into the corner of the kitchen," Mum muttered, heaving her computer up into her arms. "She's got some idea that computer screens give out radiation or something and poison the atmosphere."

I laughed, disbelieving. "I'm not joking!" grumbled Mum. "I couldn't get her to go NEAR the microwave, last time she was here. She thinks all electronic equipment is set on siphoning out your brains while you sleep."

I began to like the sound of Auntie Grace; I liked her even more when she arrived twelve hours early on Friday morning because she'd never got to grips with the twenty-four-hour clock and she'd assumed 4.00 hours was teatime. The old lady wasn't fazed; she'd just jumped in a cab soon as she realized her mistake.

"Saves you a trip to meet me, Justine!" she

beamed, before adding loudly, "Goodness, you've put on some weight."

It didn't take me long to work out just why Mum found her just so difficult as a house guest. It wasn't that she was grumpy, or difficult, or unappreciative – it was just that she had a will at least as strong as Mum's, and she was one of Nature's Anarchists. She was always a bit out of kilter, a bit out of step, with normality, and Mum couldn't bear that, because she wanted everything to be organized. Grace would go out for the day to meet some old friends, and tell Mum not to worry about feeding her in the evening. Only then she'd arrive back "a bit peckish" and insist on making pancakes which smelt so delicious that Dad, Sarah and I would congregate in the kitchen and get her to cook us some, too, while Mum tapped indignantly on her console in the corner. Then there was the day Grace insisted on repotting all Mum's house plants for her, and not only made an unholy mess on the patio but called Mum down to take note and be ticked off every time she found one that was particularly badly pot bound. "Roots need room to *grow*!" she'd say. "Same as people!"

And she had the trick of making comments that would kill conversations dead in their tracks. "Nothing was ever made better by moaning about it!" she said to Mum's depressed friend, Claire, stopping her in mid-flow. By the end of week two, Mum's friends had stopped calling at the house almost completely and Mum's smile was thin and infrequent.

I spent quite a bit of time with Auntie Grace, showing her round, taking her out for tea. At first I did it out of duty; then I realized I was enjoying her company. She made me laugh, often without meaning to, and she stirred me telling me all about the great open spaces in Canada, where you could still walk all day and not meet a soul. She told me about all the snow in winter, how great the skiing was. "And the thunderstorms!" she cried. "They're a treat. Whenever one gets up, I just drag my chair out on to the porch and watch the lightning crackling over the forest. It's a real show."

I loved the thought of that – an old lady watching a storm instead of the telly.

"Nature is so powerful," she said once. "It has the measure of us all."

I laughed and told her she sounded like my ex-boyfriend who was hooked on the sea and surfing, and before I knew it I was telling her all about him, all about the power he'd had over me. "Nature again, you see," she said. "All part of Nature. Ah, you'll get over it. You've made a sticky start, that's all – you'll meet someone else when you're ready."

I loved Art being described as a sticky start. It kind of put him in his place, somehow.

Then something phenomenal happened. We were

eating supper one night halfway through Grace's visit, when the old lady suddenly cleared her throat and announced, "I've been spending some time talking to Colette this week. Seems to me the girl's exhausted, needs a real change of scene. Working hard, getting all messed up by a member of the opposite sex. Seems to me she couldn't do better than come back with me, stay at my place for a while. I've got plenty of room. She can stay as long as she wants, as long as she's happy – till she goes off to college if she likes."

We'd all stopped eating and were gazing at Grace, open-mouthed.

"Oh, it's not a free ticket," Grace went on. "There's work she could get in Ontario – it' s only half an hour away on the bus. I know a coupla people be glad to give her work right now – bright girl, English accent. She won't need much money though. Just a bit for her keep. And I wouldn't interfere, but I'd be there to take care of her."

She put down her knife and fork and beamed round at all of us. "Wanted to tell you all together," she said. "So that neither Justine nor Coll thought I'd been plotting with the other one."

There was a long pause, then I gathered my senses and said. "Look – *thank* you, Auntie Grace. That is just the most amazing offer, I – I don't know what to say."

She turned to me. "The idea came to me when you were complaining all your friends had got fixed up, and you had no idea what to do. Well, from what you told me, you've had no time to work out what to do. Seems to me you need a break, girl."

Mum leaned across the table towards me. "A HOLIDAY would be wonderful, wouldn't it, Colette? I mean – you could go for six weeks or so – and still get back for the start of term in October. . ."

"Ach, holidays," said Grace. "They don't sort you out, just buck you up a bit. And anyway, I thought Coll said she could have a whole year off, before she goes off to college."

"I can," I said.

"And maybe it'll be the only time she'll have that freedom, just to take off, for a whole year," put in Dad, thoughtfully. "Until she gets to Grace's age, that is."

Everyone but Mum laughed. Grace sat back and said, "You think about it. I'm not interfering in your family decisions."

Her interference, of course, had already been absolute.

The more I thought about it, the more I loved it. Dad said I should go. Sarah said I should go, so she could have my attic. Mum had reservations.

"It's so isolated," she said. "I mean – I know there's a bus, but what—"

"I've still got my car, you know," Grace interrupted indignantly. "I can look after her. She needs the doctor, I can get her there."

"You still DRIVE, Auntie Grace?" asked Mum, visibly quailing.

"Certainly do. Roads over there aren't like the circus they are here. She wants to go to a late party – I can collect."

I had this bizarre vision of Grace pulling up outside a rave to give me a lift home, and I put my arm round her thin shoulders. "I'd really like to come over," I said. "The more I hear, the better it gets."

"Needn't think I'd be running round after you, though," she replied, looking pleased. "I got my garden, things to do. I still help out at the Old Folks' centre twice a week."

Mum had shut her eyes. "Grace, you ARE an Old Folk."

"Not yet I'm not. Stop worrying, Justine. I've got my strength. And I've got good neighbours, if it ever lets me down."

"Anyway, I wouldn't *want* you to look after me, Grace," I said. "Honestly." And then this fabulous feeling of hope, of things widening out, flooded into me. I thought of what she'd said about the Canadian skyline. Open, endless, vast.

"You'd have your own space," Grace was saying. "Privacy. You can have the big bedroom at the front.

Looks out over the forest. So you can see the storms from there or," she winked, "come down on to the porch with me and get yourself good and wet."

"I want to go, Mum," I said. "I really want to."

"Well," Mum began, "if that's how you feel, I suppose it's—"

"Settled," said Grace. "You may as well fly back with me. I'm sure we can get you on the same flight. Has to be an empty seat somewhere."

"Oh – NO," said Mum. "If she goes that soon she'll be away for her eighteenth birthday."

"Oh, Justine, stop fussing. Give the girl a bon voyage party before she goes, and we can celebrate her birthday back in Canada. What's the matter, think I can't bake a cake?"

Chapter thirty-four

And so it was settled. The air fare over was going to be my eighteenth birthday present from Grace; and Mum, appeased by the thought of a farewell party, said I could have my family presents then. I only had a week left before I went. Sure, going to stay in Canada with an elderly relative wasn't everyone's idea of breaking out in their gap year, but it felt right for me. It was safe, and it was somehow empty, unplanned, and that, I realized, after the year I'd just had, was what I most craved. I kept thinking of Grace saying you had to get the binoculars out to see another house. And yet Ontario, with its shops and its jobs and its nightlife, was only thirty minutes away on the bus.

It was perfect.

Mum channelled all her anxieties into arranging a going-away party for me. The weather was so hot we decided to have it at home, spilling out from the back room into the garden. I heard Mum on the phone organizing friends to make food, ordering a cake, even enquiring about garden flares.

"Stop looking so woebegone, Justine," Grace said one evening. "Your kids can't be with you for ever. Tell you what – my Christmas present this year to

Coll. A one-way ticket home, or a return – whichever she wants." Mum beamed, and I flew round the table and hugged first her, then Grace, who I'd started to look on as a rather tactless fairy godmother. She seemed to sort everything.

I phoned round everyone who wasn't away, told them my plans, and invited them to come to my party. Maggie was ecstatic, made me promise to write once I'd got to Canada, said of course she'd be at my party. Val announced she was jealous of me, but said she knew what she needed was to get immersed in a new life, new people, and work. Emptiness would do her in, she said. I asked her if she minded if I invited Greg to the party, and she took a deep breath and said, no, I had to ask him, he was part of my past, just like she was.

"Jesus, Val," I laughed. "I'm not leaving for ever. 'Part of my past' – honestly! Aren't you going to feature in my future at all?"

She laughed, and I could tell I'd pleased her. "You have to write to me," I said. "Lots. And when I get back at Christmas, we'll see each other, OK?"

From then on, my mind was full of packing and the party I was having, and I felt great. I didn't even mind when Mum announced we had to drive down and see Gwen over the weekend. "After all, Grace is *her* aunt too," she said, somewhat testily. "We'll get off straight after breakfast."

I decided to stay in Friday night. Mum's "straight after breakfast" meant something obscene, like 9.30 a.m. I thought I'd have a hot, deep bath and go to bed early. I was in the kitchen, making a mug of hot chocolate to drink in the bath, when there was a knock at the front door. I stomped out and pulled it open, expecting it to be someone for Mum – and came face to face with Art.

"Hi," he said.

"Hi," I replied. I felt like the blood had drained from my face.

"I heard you were leaving the country. I just thought I'd come and wish you good luck and stuff."

"Oh. Right."

"Well – good luck and stuff." He leaned towards me a little, smiling.

"Who told you?" I whispered. "That I was going?"

"Joe. Canada, right?"

"Yeah."

Just then, the door to the kitchen slammed, and Art jumped and backed away, as though he thought Mum might rush out with a meat cleaver. "Look – can we go somewhere?" he said. "Just for a bit. I want – to talk to you." I hesitated, and he said, "Please, Coll. Just for a bit."

"All right," I muttered. "Let me get my key."

I pushed the door to while I found my key, grabbed some money, brushed my hair, stabbed on some lipstick. Then I scuttled outside, and we set off down the road together in silence. I felt seized up with the shock of walking next to him again.

"Where shall we go?" he said. "That riverside pub?"

"OK," I said.

As we walked there he asked me about Canada and I told him, trying to keep my voice calm and level. It all sounded pretty safe and tame, compared to him just blasting off to New Zealand without knowing anyone, but he said he'd always wanted to go to Canada, and Auntie Grace sounded wild. When we got to the pub he went in to get the drinks and I sat down at a table outside and made myself breathe slowly. I tried to concentrate my brain, but I couldn't.

Art reappeared and sat down opposite me. "Here's your drink," he said. Then: "It's great to see you again."

I didn't answer, just forced myself to meet his eyes.

"Come on, Coll, don't look so frosty. I did what you wanted, didn't I? I didn't try to get in touch with you – not till you'd got through your exams. How'd you do anyway?"

"The results aren't out yet."

"But d'you think you did OK?"

"Yeah. Good enough to get to York." Then I croaked out a laugh. "You saying you *wanted* to get in touch with me?"

"Yeah."

There was a long pause. "Why?" I asked.

Art shrugged. "I just did. I mean – you run out on me – then you send me this drama queen letter – it was all still hanging for me, like *I* didn't have a say in anything."

I could feel my head nodding slowly, angrily. "Right. You didn't. Not then."

"OK, I didn't."

"It was about *survival* for me."

"God, Coll, you always—"

"You'd done enough damage. I wasn't about to let you make me screw up my exams too."

"OK, OK. Look – I respected what you said in that letter. That's why I waited."

I glared down into my glass. "Are you expecting me to say thank you or something?"

"What?"

"Because I'm not going to."

"Jesus, Coll, what are you being so *spiky* for? I only want to talk."

"OK, then. Go ahead and talk."

"Well, there's not much point, is there, if you're going to be like this –"

I looked up, and saw his face all sort of offended and bewildered, and I felt this amazing, liberating rage rip through me. "Oh, for *fuck's sake*, Art, what d'you expect me to be like? All nice and *chatty*.

You've just about smashed up my life over the last year. You – you *take me over*, then you dump me, and I feel like I'm going to *die*, then you *come back*, and try to make out we're just friends, well, we're *not*, are we? The last time we *saw* each other proved that. Maybe you've *forgotten*?"

I threw myself back in my chair and glared at him. He looked shaken, then after a few seconds this smile started just at the corners of his mouth. "Of course I haven't forgotten," he said. "I'd been wanting to do that with you ever since I got back."

"Don't pull that on me," I said, weakly. "Just – don't."

"Look, Coll, you're not the only one with feelings."

"Aren't I? Well, you're so bloody good at hiding yours, I wouldn't know. If you knew the *state* I've been in –"

"I know, I know. I'm sorry."

"And then you just *turn up* again, and act as though nothing's happened –"

"Look – why d'you *think* I turned up? Why d'you think I went away in the first place?"

"I don't know. 'Cos you're a bastard."

"Because I cracked up. At college, I cracked up. I missed you so much I felt – I can't tell you how I felt. And the way we split up it was – *awful.* I spent hours just going over it in my head, wondering why I let it happen. I couldn't stand it. I couldn't speak to anyone there. It was all fake. I felt like I was walking around and everyone else was on a different planet. I just wanted to get drunk and sleep."

There was a silence. I felt like my heart had stopped. "So why didn't you call me," I whispered.

"*Call* you? It scared the shit out of me. I just wanted to get out, break with everything."

"OK. So if you wanted to break with everything, why get in touch when you got back?"

"You saying you didn't want me to?"

"I'm not – I didn't – oh, shit. I'm saying it was weird, the way we started acting like we were only friends, like. . ."

"That's what it was, Coll. Acting."

"You're saying you were acting?"

"Yeah. Course I was. I didn't know what you wanted. I didn't know what you felt about me. Not after what had happened. . ."

"You could have just told me what *you* felt." That night – in the bedroom – you could've *said* something. There was a long pause. "OK, no you couldn't. Beyond you, right?"

Art half groaned, half laughed. "Yeah, beyond me. And I didn't know what I felt. I hated feeling that bad about you, it really did my head in, Coll, it really messed me up. . ."

"Good."

"Cow."

"*No*. I just want to know it wasn't all on my side, it wasn't just *me* feeling, it was there, you know? It was real, what we had."

"Yes, it was. It *is*."

I stared at him. "What?"

"It's just – it's just – when I heard you were going to Canada, I just about – I freaked. I'm scared. I'm scared of losing you. You remember when we split up? And you said something about being scared, you know, that you'd never meet anyone else to . . . anyone else to. . ."

"Come up to you. Yes."

"Well . . . that's what I feel. Now."

I sat and soaked up those words and part of me was dancing in joy and triumph and part of me wanted to snatch up his beer glass and break it over his head.

"Art –" I took in a deep breath. "I've been waiting for you to say this *all year*. All the time we were together, and all the time you were in New Zealand, and then when you got back – it's been all I've wanted."

"Well I've said it, Coll. If I had you back now, I'd never let you go."

Those corny words – they were like treacle, honey, trickling all through me, sealing up all the wounds and cracks inside me. I shut my eyes and said, "I'm going in six days' time."

"I know. I know you are."

"And I think part of the reason you're saying this is because you know I'm going."

"*What?*"

"I'm going, so it's safe to say it, Art."

He looked at me silently, mortally offended. I laughed, and after a minute, he laughed too. "OK, OK," he said. "Maybe you have a point. But I mean it, too. I do."

I looked down at the table, and he leaned over and said, "Let me come with you."

"No."

"Stay behind then, come with me to college. I'm doing that ocean studies course I told you about. I'll work nights – I'll keep you."

"Stop it, you wanker."

"Coll, seriously."

"If I said yes you'd be out of the door faster than –"

He reached over, got hold of my hand, squeezed it. "I wouldn't. I swear I wouldn't. Don't you want me any more?"

"You know what I want? I want to kill you."

"OK."

"Slowly."

"OK."

"Painfully."

"You see – you still love me."

"Yeah, I do. Just about. But I'm still going away, *alone*, OK?"

"Can't I even come and see you?" he said, and squeezed my hand again.

I felt it right through me. I had this sudden vision of us lying wrapped up together on a bed, watching a storm beat against the window. "Maybe," I said.

"I could get the money together. For the air fare."

"Look, Art. What I want right now is a break, OK? From all that – *feeling*. I want space, and I want somewhere new, and I'm only just realizing now how young I am, and I don't want to start making plans and promises and crap."

"It's just – suppose we're right for each other. I mean really right. I mean I've felt more for you than – *anyone* else."

"Art – you've probably never felt anything for anyone else."

"That's not true."

"Well anyway – if we *are* right, there's no need to grab at it, is there? It'll keep."

"OK. I'll wait."

"Sure you will. Right through university."

He looked at me. "Yeah."

"Get real, Art."

"I am real. Will you give me your address in Canada?"

"I don't know. Oh, *Art*! You're being a complete

234

shit, talking like this. You know I'm still crazy about you, you know it, and it's – sitting here with you like this, your *face* –"

He grinned. "What about my face?"

"Oh, *shut up.*" I was smiling back at him, I couldn't help it, and I could feel my eyes getting all wet.

"I hate to think of you – you know. Sleeping with someone else."

"That's too bad. With your track record, it's not only too bad, it's a huge *joke* –"

"Yeah, yeah." Art picked up his beer and downed it and said, "What about us?"

"What?"

"One last time?"

"Go screw yourself."

He laughed, and went to get some more drinks. When he got back, I said, "Art, I'm getting the weirdest feeling of *déja vu.*"

"Yeah?" He sounded hopeful.

"Yeah. We've done this before, haven't we? When we split up before. It's like you can only be open when we've had some kind of bust-up."

He looked at me, wary, and I went on, "Grace told me this great story. That we're all a house with four rooms."

"*What?*"

"One room is emotions, one is physical, one is

235

mental, one is – the last is spiritual. And everyone has their favourite rooms they spend most of their time in but you're only a real complete human being if you visit each room, every day."

"Coll, what on earth are you on about?"

"I'm not so sure about the spiritual, although Grace reckons that can be stuff like Nature, so maybe I'm OK. But I reckon I visit the other three lots. Whereas you – hours in physical, the odd half hour in mental. Spiritual, maybe, when you're getting off on the sea. Emotional – barred and locked. Opened only in crisis."

"Don't give me that *shit*, Coll."

"It's true. Your physical room – it's like a *gym*, with a bar in the corner, and a big screen to watch football, and—"

"Yeah? Well you live in your sodding emotional room, OK? It's squishy and soft with that crap music you like playing loud and *pillows* everywhere and—"

"Shut up, Art," I said, laughing. "I'm the balanced one, face it. You're a psycho."

"Don't go away, Coll."

"I'm going."

"We're good together, you know we are. Who else can you have this with?"

"If it's that good, it'll last. Till you grow up a bit. Now shut up. I'm going.

"Can I come to your party?"

"What?"

"Your going-away party. Joe told me."

"Oh, *Art*. No, you can't. I don't trust you. More to the point, I don't trust *me*."

He lowered his head and grinned at me. "I s'pose that's something," he said.

Soon after that we finished our drinks and I stood up to go and said he shouldn't see me home. He asked me again for my address in Canada and I told him I'd write to him at Joe's once I got there. Then I resisted kissing him goodbye and resisted saying anything like "see you at Christmas" and walked off with my head down without looking back.

Chapter thirty-five

All the rest of that evening something warm and strong flowed into me, like having a blood transfusion. I remembered everything he'd said, and I felt made over, made new. It had been real, that love we'd had. Just as real for him.

It was weird, I lost myself in dreamy fantasies about how Art and I kept in touch and got back together years on down the line, but I never had any doubts about going away. I had to go, or I knew I'd get all out of balance again. If I stayed with him now – he'd stop my life somehow. I couldn't explain it.

We set off for Auntie Gwen's next day, Dad doing the driving, Great Auntie Grace cheerfully squashed between me and Sarah in the back seat. Gwen was so pleased and welcoming when we arrived she verged on the hysterical. She'd made us a massive lunch, and she opened wine and Grace got tiddly and dozed off which allowed Mum and Gwen to discuss her in intense, low-pitched voices. I went for a walk along the beach with Tess the mad dog, and felt supremely content. Not even getting back to Gwen's in the early evening and discovering I had to share my bedroom with Sarah could spoil it.

The next day I got up early, threw open the bedroom window, and realized that autumn had arrived, with its soft bite in the mornings, its low, ageing sun in the afternoons. Usually at this time, when the first leaves start to turn, I feel a sense of desperation that I haven't wrung enough out of the summer yet, a sense of panic that yet another new term is about to start.

But this year was different. This year the autumn signalled my freedom.

Grace was yelling up the stairs about an early morning walk along the beach and how she'd cook us all pancakes when we got back. Sarah burrowed deeper into her sleeping bag and I shouted that I was coming. I pulled on my swimming costume, then jeans and a sweatshirt, grabbed a towel, and raced downstairs.

Grace had managed to chivvy Mum into coming along too, so the three of us set out along the cliff path and down to the beach. I looked at the waves, low, white, endlessly arriving. "I hope you're going in," said Grace. "I hope you haven't brought that towel along for nothing."

I crouched down on the shoreline and trailed my fingers in the water. "It's not that cold," I said.

"It will be if you IMMERSE yourself in it," said Mum. "Be sensible, Colette. Don't you get enough swimming at home?"

Grace grinned at me wickedly, and I grinned back and peeled off my sweatshirt. "It's had all summer to warm up," I said. Then I kicked off my shoes and stripped off my jeans, and walked into the waves.

The shock as it came over my waist almost sent me back to the shore again, but I couldn't, not with Mum standing there waiting to be proved right. I took a deep breath, and threw myself forward, and started breaststroking along. As my body got used to the cold I laughed aloud and turned and waved triumphantly at the shore. "It's great!" I yelled.

"Don't go too far out!" Mum bellowed.

I headed out for a few more metres, then I started swimming parallel to the shore. Waves were coming at me, wave on wave, and I threw myself over them like a hurdler, surging up, coasting down.

The greyness was immense. Grey all the way out to the horizon; lighter grey where the sky met the sea. There were no boundaries, not like the swimming pool. No lanes, keeping you in a straight line. And I needed a lot more strength, and a lot more stamina; yet at the same time I was held up, floating.

I can cope, I thought. *I* can. You've got no say in a lot of the things life throws at you – but you do have a say in how you deal with those things. How you let them affect you. How you let them change you, inside.

A light rain started pattering on the surface of the

sea, and I trod water for a minute and raised my face to it. Then I started swimming again, moving forward, somewhere between the horizon and the shoreline, in rhythm with the waves.

Diving In

Coll loves to swim – diving into the clear blue water makes her feel free. Much freer than it's possible to at home, with her larger-than-life mother and her mother's needy friends cluttering up the kitchen table.

There's also the boy Coll keeps seeing at the pool – he's gorgeous and swims like a shark. She knows she doesn't stand a chance but there's no harm in fantasizing about him, what it would be like to be with him…

Then, one chlorine-filled Thursday night, it happens. He asks her out. And so begins a passionate love-affair which finds Coll well and truly in at the deep end…

In the Deep End

Coll has just about forgiven Art for assuming that she'll sleep with him. He's promised her that they can take things slowly, that the time has to be right for her. But just when is "the right time"? And how will their relationship change afterwards?

There's only one way to find out. Coll is about to plunge into the first truly passionate relationship of her life and she's excited, scared, exhilarated...
But will she sink, or swim?

Praise for the *Diving In* trilogy:

"A good meaty read – an intelligent book with intelligent characters"

THE TIMES

"Some of the best writing about love and sex that I have ever read in a book for young people ... both emotionally stunning and morally unshakeable"

BOOKS FOR KEEPS

Look out for *Diving In* and *Sink or Swim*